The
Absolutely
Perfect Horse

The
Absolutely
Perfect Horse

by Marylois Dunn
with Ardath Mayhar

1 8  1 7

HARPER & ROW, PUBLISHERS

Cambridge, Philadelphia, San Francisco, London, Mexico City, São Paulo, Sydney

NEW YORK

Library of Congress Cataloging in Publication Data
Dunn, Mary Lois.
   The absolutely perfect horse.

   Summary: The formerly noble, now downtrodden horse known as Dogmeat helps Annie
and her family reassess their values.
   1. Horses—Juvenile fiction. [1. Horses—Fiction]
I. Mayhar, Ardath.   II. Title.
PZ10.3.D883Ab 1983   [Fic]   82-47726
ISBN 0-06-021773-1
ISBN 0-06-021774-X (lib. bdg.)

The
Absolutely
Perfect Horse

1

The bill of sale said his name was Admiral Benbow. Nobody could ever figure out why, for he was never called that. The sideshow people called him Chief, to make him seem truly an Indian pony. I called him Dogmeat, for by the time he came to us that was all he was good for. And it was a more appropriate name for the bony old Appaloosa than my sister would ever admit.

He backed out of the trailer as confidently as if he were coming home, and later I realized that it was true. The old horse had found a home, at last . . . a home to die in. But first he made himself so much a part of the Braeden family that he will live as long as the last of us lives. Dogmeat was a different sort of horse.

He arrived late in the spring of the year I turned thirteen. By the time my birthday rolled around, I had aged a long way past any thirteen, and Annie, my fifteen-year-old sister, had grown up overnight. Looking back, I really don't understand how we had remained as childlike as we had, for there had been sudden and dramatic changes in our lives already.

The change had begun abruptly. Lieutenant Commander Kelley had come, himself, with the telegram announcing that our father had been badly injured while on duty in the Far East. Commander Kelley was a special friend of our family, and Annie and I had called him Uncle Ed ever since we could remember. We were lucky that that was so, because he didn't stop at breaking the news gently to us and Mother— he arranged to have Dad flown to the big hospital in Honolulu. Then he got Mother transport to go over and take care of him.

Not content with all that, he took us home with him, and we stayed there and went to school with his children for five months. That was a long five months. We seemed to be suspended somewhere unfamiliar, just going to school, then rushing home to see if there was a letter from Mom. I can still feel the warm glow I felt when she wrote, "Your father took a couple of steps today—all by himself."

Her letters were full of all kinds of interesting things as well as news of her patient. She loved the islands and the people there, and she had known a lot of them before, when she and Dad had been stationed there. Mostly, though, she wrote about the boy who had saved Dad's life when his small boat had hit an old mine—heaven knows which war it was from—that had somehow gotten itself out into the river.

Taro Chan was the boy's name, but he wasn't Japanese. He was Vietnamese, actually, though his name had somehow come out as Japanese. Uncle Ed laughed when he said the name and told us it was the equivalent of John Doe in America. It was a funny name, but that was all I could see about him that was funny. You could tell from Mom's letters that she liked him a lot. When Taro Chan recovered from his wounds, and the government was going to ship him back to Thailand, where he and Dad had been hurt, she and Dad did a lot of talking and yelling and medal rattling. It was arranged that Taro Chan would stay on in Honolulu.

Mom came home plumper and rounder than I remembered. She was quick to wrap us in hugs, and I had to reach farther than ever before to get my arms around her.

"That's because there's going to be a baby," she said.

Annie was tickled to death. She was full of plans, right off. "We can take that little playroom and put all Petey's junk in the attic," she started.

"It's not junk, but you can put most of it away if you want to," I said. I really didn't care. Most of the stuff was toys I didn't have time for anymore. The games and things I really wanted could be stuffed under my bed or in the closet. I had a lot of old motorcycle magazines I could throw out to make room.

Mom sat down on the couch and patted the cushions on either side of her. We sat close, so she could hug and sit at the same time.

"The baby won't be the only new member of the family," she said. "Sam and I have decided to adopt Taro Chan. Most of the paperwork is already done, and we hope he can come home with your dad when he flies home."

I couldn't work up a lot of excitement about a little squally baby, as Annie could. Babies seem to interest girls a lot, I've noticed. Taro Chan was something else. A full-grown brother to play with! Though I wasn't sure, from what Mom had written, that he'd know very much about playing. He was no older than Annie, but he'd been a sailor in the Thai river fleet for several years already. He had fought Reds and even river pirates, she said. He could handle a boat as well as any man, and, to quote Dad, he "could come on real warlike when the occasion demanded." It would be something to have a Vietnamese brother, and a warrior, besides.

"We can put bunk beds in my room," I said. I was already planning to begin clearing out my room to make space . . . maybe that very afternoon.

"Well . . ." Mom sounded thoughtful. Her eyes

were hiding something from us, as if she were wondering how much news we could take all at the same time. "I don't think we'll worry too much about changing this house. We won't be living here much longer."

"Are we being transferred?" Annie asked. I don't ever remember being transferred. We had been when I was little, but we'd lived in this house for eight years, and it was all I could remember.

"Not transferred," Mom said. "Your father is going to retire from the Navy. He had some bad wounds and a lot of surgery. He can't handle anything but a desk job anymore, and that would kill him more surely than the mine almost did. You know him. If he's not out doing something active, he's miserable."

"But we own this house," Annie said. There was a quaver in her voice. "We'll have to change schools."

"I'm afraid so. Still, you'll finish out the year here and start the new school in September, so it isn't like beginning in the middle of a year. And houses can be sold as well as bought."

"Where are we going to move to?" I asked. I was doing my best to keep my own voice from quivering. I had never gone to school anywhere but here, and I didn't think I was going to like changing very much. From her expression, Annie wasn't either.

"Petey, you may not remember, but Annie does, I know. We used to go to Texas every summer to visit my mother and father on the farm." She looked at Annie, who nodded and tried to smile. Mom hugged her again. "That was a long time ago. When

Mother died, a year after my father, she left the farm to me. We've rented the land to tenants, but the old house is just like Mother left it."

"But a farm . . ." Annie was concerned. "Won't that be awfully hard work for Dad?"

"It's hard work," Mom agreed. "Sam may not be able to do the heavy work for a long time. Maybe not the hardest of it . . . ever. But if all of us pitch in, with Taro Chan and a good hired hand I think we can make it work. I used to be pretty good at keeping a vegetable garden and tending chickens and pitching hay, when I was a girl. I'll bet you don't know that I can still milk a cow!"

We both laughed.

"Mother," Annie said, "you never wear jeans, even. We have always had a maid. I didn't know you could do anything."

"Except cook," I interrupted. "You sure can cook good!"

Mom laughed with us, this time. "And can vegetables and make preserves and jellies. I can make quilts and our own soap, find wild things to eat and to cure illnesses with. Not to mention hunt quail and dress chickens for eating and a thousand country things you've never had a chance to do. It's going to be fun for us all."

I didn't think "fun" sounded like quite the word for it, but Mom sounded so eager for us to like her idea that it would have been impossible not to try to.

"What kind of farm is it?" I asked. We had studied

8

a bit about different kinds of farming in Social Studies.

"It used to be a dairy farm, when my father was alive," Mother said. "It's good pasture land, good hayfields. You know, your father was raised on a ranch in North Dakota. He knows a lot about cattle. Sam thinks we can start out and build a beef herd. It takes a while to begin making money out of it, but it's pretty steady once the income starts coming in and the herd is built up and self-sustaining. And it isn't nearly as physically demanding as most other kinds of farming. Not so much equipment is needed, either. That can run into money if you don't watch it."

"It'll be more like a ranch than a farm," Annie said. She smiled for the first time . . . a real smile, I mean. "Horses. There will have to be horses to work the cattle."

"Perhaps later. It's not like a big open range, Annie. There are only six hundred and forty acres, all broken up into fenced pastures. Sam will probably use a jeep or a tractor to take care of the livestock."

Annie's smile faded, and her face slid into lines of disappointment. "But I don't know why you couldn't have a riding horse," Mom added quickly.

Annie forgot all about changing schools and laying aside all her old friends. "Oh, Mom, really? A black horse with a white star and white stockings? That would be an Absolutely Perfect Horse!"

Seeing Annie bounce around on her end of the couch didn't surprise me very much. A horse of her own was Annie's dream. She read books about horses, went to movies about horses, collected pictures, maga-

9

zines, and little statues of horses. The last time I counted, there were one hundred and eighty-three of the little statues. A hundred and eighty-four, if you counted the big jade horse Mom kept under the glass dome in the living room. It was really Annie's, but it was too precious to be hidden away upstairs.

Annie went away to camp in the summers so she could ride every day. When Mom took us to the park so Annie could ride, it always looked to me as if she rode at least as well as most of the TV cowboys.

"Well, I would rather have an absolutely perfect motorcycle, like a 750 Harley or BSA. Slightly used, of course," I butted in.

Mom gave us another squeeze. "If that's what it will take to make you happy, we'll see what can be done. It's a big thing to move away from everything, everyone you have ever known." She paused a moment, thinking. "You know, you'll have to be reasonable about things. Annie, you may never find a horse with those absolutely perfect markings. And Petey, if we could afford a cycle like that, you aren't big enough to handle it yet."

We both nodded. That was reasonable. Still, I could feel Mom working up to something else. The Zinger.

"You know how expensive everything is, what with inflation. The move is going to be a terrible strain on our resources." I nodded, and I could see Annie nodding, too. She felt the Zinger coming as well as I did.

"We'll be able to sell this house for a lot of money, but the old farmhouse will have to be fixed up a lot.

It has a huge attic that we plan to divide into two large bedrooms and a bath for you boys. The house will have to be reroofed, painted inside and out. New appliances, new plumbing . . . even new wiring will have to go into it.

"And that's only the house. The fences are all old and will have to be repaired or rebuilt entirely. So will the barn and the sheds. There will have to be a certain amount of new equipment, too, and with the cost of the livestock, that will take a bundle. Can you imagine the money that's going to cost us?"

"Lots!" I said.

"Do we have enough?" Annie asked doubtfully.

"Not to do everything all at once," Mom answered in a reassuring voice. "But once we sell this house, then with our savings, we can make a good start on the important things. First the house, making it livable, and then the livestock. The rest will come along, in time. Not too long, I should think."

"I have lots of money in the bank," I reminded her.

"Me, too," Annie said.

"Not your college money." Mom shook her head decidedly. "We aren't going to touch that. It will be more important than ever to leave your money alone. College will be coming up soon enough for you two, and you'll need everything you have, plus anything we can add to it. And Taro Chan will have to have a chance to go to school, too. Money is going to be a little short around here for a while."

Annie frowned. "If we don't have any money to

spend, how can we get Petey a cycle and me a horse?"

"Why, you already get an allowance. And when you work on the farm, you'll be paid for that, too. We don't tell you how to spend your allowances, and we won't tell you how to spend your salaries. If you want to spend what you get, fine. If you want to save for what you want, then that's even better."

"Wow!" I said. "I never made a salary before."

"Well, it won't be as much as a full-time, full-grown hired man would make, because you will be part owner of the farm, and you'll be working for yourselves, just as your father and I will. Still, it'll be a substantially larger amount than you're getting now."

"What about him?" Annie said, and I knew she meant Taro Chan. "Will he get an allowance too?"

"Of course," Mom answered. "Remember, Taro Chan is your adopted brother. You have to start thinking of him as a member of the family, not as an outsider. He's going to feel strange enough as it is, when he comes home."

I hugged her again. "I'm glad you decided to take him into the family," I said, hoping that she didn't notice that Annie just sniffed and didn't say a thing.

2

That was the day, I remember, when I started really thinking before I bought a comic book. *Do I want this now or a motorcycle later?* It had never occurred to me before to save money for one, because Mom would never have let me have one in the city. No more than she could let Annie have a horse on our roof garden.

That day, too, marked a change in Mom. Instead of deciding instantly, when Annie or I asked her about anything, she began to say, "We'll have to wait and ask your father." It seemed a little strange, for Dad had been gone a long time, and we were used to having Mom make all the decisions.

After a while, I figured that it was her way of easing

us into the habit of looking to Dad as well as to her for answers to our questions. Besides that, it was hard not to get the feeling that there were going to be a lot more changes coming about in our lives . . . aside from a big move and two new members added to the family.

The changes began with Dad's return. That was like a new beginning for everybody. He stood tall and straight in the door of the plane. Then he stepped slowly and carefully down the ramp to the spot where we waited. I could feel him controlling the need to limp. There was something about the set of his shoulders, the way he moved, that told me he was hurting. But he didn't limp, just made straight for us.

The ground was wet from showers that had fallen the night before, and everything smelled fresh and clean. Dad's uniform was as crisp as if it had just come off the hanger, and sunlight glittered on the gold trim and the clusters of ribbons on his chest. He was so thin; I didn't remember him as being so terribly thin. His smile was the same, though, curved like a sailing sea gull's wings.

He hugged and kissed Mom and Annie, then he held out his hand to me. I took it, and we shook hands, but I wanted to be hugged too, so I wrapped my arms around his waist, and he held me tighter than anyone else. Then he turned, one arm still heavy around my shoulders, and held out his free hand to the slim Oriental youth who had come down the ramp behind him.

"Annie, Petey, this is Taro Chan."

Strangely, I felt disappointed. From his name and the things Mom had told us in her letters . . . about what a soldier he was . . . I expected Taro Chan to be a Samurai sort of person. This slender, dark-eyed boy with the shy smile looked not very different from the boys in my class. His name didn't fit, either. There was nothing Japanese about him, unless it was his eyes. They were definitely Oriental, but the rest of him, face and all, was just like ordinary people.

"The Captain says I have good English," he said, holding out his hand to me. "I am please to becoming your brother."

He pronounced brother as "brudder," the way the Hawaiians did when they were talking to tourists. I didn't know if he always talked that way or if he was teasing. I took his hand anyway.

"Your English is good enough for us. It's going to be great to have another man on my side. I've always been outvoted by the women up to now."

Taro Chan looked with distress at Mom and Annie. "I do not think it is ever correct I should argue with the mother," he said.

Dad and I laughed, and Mother nodded. "You'll learn, my lad, when you've been around Annie and Petey for a while. You'll learn how, I'd bet on it." She kissed him on the cheek, and he blushed.

"You'll have to get used to that," I told him. "Mom's a hugger and kisser."

"I think I can get used to," he answered very seri-

15

ously. "I think I will like very much a hugger and kisser. It has been very long since my own mother is gone."

"Is she dead?" Annie asked, speaking to him for the first time.

"There is no way to know," he said. "I am very young when the war in Vietnam is over. My village is gone, I am left too young to know anything. The Americans find me, give me into care of nuns. They take me to Thailand. One of sisters was Japanese, Sister Toyoko. She name me Taro Chan, because I was too young to know my name. They give me home, while I am little. When I was older, I joined the river patrol. And that is how I met the Captain. Your father."

I could tell that he had rehearsed that speech many times. He would have realized that we would be curious about his past. Still, he seemed embarrassed. "I think I have answered more question than you have asked," he mumbled.

Dad shook him affectionately by the arm. "I think you saved yourself a lot of explaining. They'd have asked you questions all the way home, if I know those two. Now that's behind you. We can get on now to important things, like what's for lunch?"

As we walked back to the station wagon, Annie always kept Mother between herself and Taro Chan. Funny, I knew she didn't like the idea of adopting him, though she hadn't said a word after Mom broke the news. I know Annie pretty well. Still, I hadn't thought she was going to be afraid of him, and that was the way she was acting.

16

When we had a minute to ourselves at home, I asked her about it.

"I don't know, Pete." She seemed miserable and strange. "I can't explain it. I'm not exactly afraid of him, but he makes my skin crawl. I wish Dad hadn't brought him."

"Annie, he didn't have anyplace else to go except back to Thailand to get killed, sooner or later, on the river. And he did save Dad's life."

She shrugged and sighed. "I know that. I can't understand it, myself. Much less explain it to you. I just don't like him."

I could think of a lot of reasons to like Taro Chan, but it isn't any use arguing with feelings. They don't understand words.

"O.K.," I said. "Can you just be nice to him?"

"I'll try, Petey. I'll really try. But will you do something for me? Just keep him a good way from me until I have time to get used to having him around. Keep him busy."

Annie need not have worried. Time and the move across four states kept us too busy to think about anything except what to pack (or unpack) next. Unless you have moved, pulled up roots and shaken loose from everything you've ever known, leaving as exciting a city as San Francisco for a run-down farm in a pine forest, you would never understand the next few weeks we lived through.

If it hadn't been for Taro Chan—T.C., as he came to be called—we wouldn't have made it. He knew what to pack and where to put it as well as Mom and Dad did. We were all the time asking, "Where should this go? Does this need to be marked fragile?" He knew, without asking. And finally the movers loaded up the boxes and crates and hauled them away, while we followed at a more leisurely pace in the station wagon.

We managed to survive it all. The new sort of life; the old/new house; the baby, who came a bit sooner than he was expected. The small new schools, when September came, were not very different from the old schools, except for their looks. The new people were mixed—I guess most people are. Not only did we survive, it even seemed that Annie might be getting over her feelings about T.C.

Among all the rest, we were saving our money, remembering Mom's promise. And in the spring, Annie announced, "Daddy, I think I'm ready to buy my horse."

3

I woke up that morning as soon as Annie's feet hit the floor in her room across the hall. I didn't move, or open my eyes. I lay with all my senses alert to what was happening all around me, as T.C. had taught me to do. I was thankful all over again that we had kept the old farmhouse instead of tearing it down to build something in brick and plastic. The old cypress house communicated. It creaked and rattled in a different way to the step of each of us. It sounded different to the beat of a south wind, north, east, and west wind. It had its sunny-day sounds and its rainy-day sounds. It was full of special noises, all comfortable, settled-down sounds.

In a strange way, it was like the house we had left

in San Francisco. Not in looks. That had been a tall, narrow house right on the street. That house had always reminded me of a tall lady wearing a jaunty flowered hat, for the flowers in the roof garden always spilled over the railings, making ruffles of color that could be seen from the street. That had been a great house, with its view of the old orange bridge and the bay. I couldn't remember another. But this was a good house, too, full of Texas's past. If it had ghosts, they were friendly ones and didn't inflict any troubles they might have had on the new tenants.

The house was waking up. I could hear Dad's razor buzzing and the sound of his voice talking to the baby in mostly nonsense talk. I heard Annie go back to her room from the bathroom, and I swung down from the top bunk and carefully set one foot in the middle of T.C.

"*Uhff!*" he grunted. That was followed by what I took to be a choice Oriental obscenity, one of those he always refused to translate and that always made Dad's eyebrows go up when T.C. forgot and let loose in his hearing.

"Petey! What for you waking me up before the birds quit singing?"

"Annie's up. Come on! You want to come along, don't you?"

T.C. narrowed his eyes into slits, making him look like Confucius. "Not me, Petey. I saw all the horses I ever wanted to see last night. It was way after midnight when we got home. This is Saturday. Just leave, very quiet. Let the old man sleep in peace." He didn't,

I noticed, have much accent anymore unless he affected it.

"Peace, brudder," I said and yanked the covers over his head before going into the bathroom to pull on my jeans and the faded pink University of Southern California sweat shirt I was going to wear. Annie didn't particularly want either one of us to go along, I well knew, but I wasn't about to miss the auction or the chance to help her pick out the Absolutely Perfect Horse.

Downstairs in the kitchen, Mom rattled pots and pans, singing as she made breakfast. Dad's voice interrupted her, and she answered with a report of the correct time. I couldn't help laughing. The electricity must have gone off again. I could imagine Dad grumbling under his breath and saying that things just weren't run shipshape in the country. Not like he was used to in the Navy, at any rate. Of course, he usually finished up his grumbling with some tale of a colossal foul-up from his underwater-demolition-team days in the Korean War.

"Now there," he would say with his eyes sparkling with memory, "was a *real* mess."

It took Annie longer to dress, painting on an inch of black goop around her eyes and straightening her nice curly hair with one of those gunks the girls use, so I went on downstairs.

"Morning, Mom. Dad. Morning, Brad." I kissed the baby on top of his head and slid onto my place on the long bench behind the table. The baby squealed "Pee-Tee" in his high, wispy voice.

Mom turned from the bacon she was frying and smiled at both of us. "Morning, Petey. Go get the paper for me, will you?"

I slid out from behind the table and closed the kitchen door quietly behind me. I took two giant steps across the wide porch and one down the three wooden steps to the path. The yard just around the house was fenced. Beds of flowers bloomed everywhere inside the fence. Ouside, the tall grass was neatly mowed on both sides of the dusty road that curved away to meet the farm-to-market road where our mailbox and the paper box stood beside our gate. Our dirt road was a good quarter mile long, and a thick stand of trees filled the curve between our place and the main road. Sometimes there were owls in the trees early in the morning. Today, except for a mockingbird and a couple of cardinals, there was nothing. The small birds wouldn't have been singing if the owl had been around.

I picked up the paper and jogged back, puffing harder than was really necessary.

"Gracious me," Dad said with a quavery voice, as I puffed into the kitchen, "you are certainly out of condition, little boy. What we need around here is a mule and a plow. That would put some muscles into those weak and spindly little legs of yours."

"Uh-huh." I continued to puff, even though the need had passed. "Maybe Annie will buy us a good mule today, instead of that A.P.H. of hers."

Dad grinned and shook out the paper. "Not a chance, Petey, my lad. You can forget about that!"

"Now don't open that paper before you eat your eggs," Mom said, turning from the stove.

Annie came bounding down the stairs, sounding almost like the horse she had talked about so constantly. Brad began to beat on his chair, chanting, "Ann-ee, Ann-ee, Ann-ee!" as soon as he heard her coming.

She picked him up and whirled him around, hugging him tightly and planting a loud kiss on top of his red curls as she plopped him back into his high chair. He squealed with delight, bouncing up and down. Dad spared a hand from the paper to steady the chair.

"Brad thinks you look especially nice this morning, too," he said, grinning at Annie as she sat down.

"Flatterers!" she laughed. "The whole lot of you."

"I didn't say a word," I said, and she wrinkled her nose at me. It didn't hurt her looks any. Annie was a pretty girl. Her hair was an exact cross between Dad's black and Mom's red, which is a hard color to describe, but nice.

She tried all the tricks to make it smooth and straight as a string, the way the Pine Hill girls wore theirs, but she never quite succeeded. The natural waves would spring out, whatever she did. This morning she had parted it in the middle and tied the heavy falls on either side with leather thongs, Indian fashion. With the loose-sleeved shirt and cutoffs and Indian moccasins, Annie looked a little like an Indian girl. Too, she hadn't taken time to paint around her eyes. They looked like two regular eyes today, instead of two sapphires in a coal bin. She was wearing pale frosted lipstick, though, and I couldn't let that pass.

"Yecch! You look like a ghoul."

She stuck out her tongue, thought how childish that must look, and settled for a haughty frown. Dad's face took on the expression he had when he didn't want us to know he was laughing at us.

"Well, my little chickadee," he said in his famous (bad) imitation of W.C. Fields. "Ready to go?"

"I've been ready for days." Annie laughed, helping herself to eggs off the platter Mom set in front of her.

"Weeks," Mom corrected, kissing her on top of the head. "I haven't heard anything but horse, horse, horse, until I think we're all going to turn into horses."

"Oh, Mom!"

Dad laughed. "Altogether, I don't think Annie's mentioned horse but every other breath since she finally scrounged enough money for the A.P.H."

Mom finally sat down at the table and looked around. "Where's T.C.?"

"He said he'd seen enough horses at the show last night to last him awhile. He wants to sleep late, so he's not coming," I said.

Annie looked at her plate and continued eating.

"He told me last night that he had a lot of history to study today," Dad said, looking at Annie. When she didn't say anything, he sighed. "I guess it's just as well."

"Well, I can't imagine T.C. being very interested

in horses," Mom said. "Now if we were going after a motorcycle . . ."

Annie looked up and grinned across the table. "A tricycle for Petey, you mean."

I threatened her with a piece of buttered toast and had her laughing again. It seemed like a good idea to keep her in a good mood, since I knew she didn't really want me tagging along, either.

I watched as Annie sat chewing somewhat mechanically, her eyes glazed, as she went off into some part of her dream about the A.P.H. Probably the part where they were galloping, wild and free. Drumming swiftly over the little-used dirt roads, having adventures, just girl and horse. She had told me her dream often enough.

"Hey," Dad said for the third time before he finally got through to her. When her eyes unglazed, he said, "Your plate's been clean for ten minutes. We're ready whenever you are."

"Now!" She got to her feet eagerly. "I'm ready right now. Meet you at the truck."

There was no doubt about her excitement. When she came outside, clutching her purse, she climbed into the middle of the pickup seat without arguing about who was going to sit on the outside. I knew by that that she was excited. Mom stood away from the truck after Dad kissed her good-bye, and waved as we headed out toward the road. The single-horse trailer we had borrowed from the vet, Dr. Kurt, bounced easily behind.

As the pickup moved across the cattle guard and onto the hard-top road, Annie began to shiver. I had had those, too, at times. The kind of shivers that start at the front of your ribs and slide all the way down to your knees, one after the other. Dad felt them, too.

"Cold, Annie?"

"Gosh no. Scared, I guess."

Dad laughed, more sympathetic than amused, and shook his head. "I know the feeling."

Now that we were this far down the road, I decided it was safe to become a speaking member of the group. "After seeing all those gaited horses and those jumpers last night, what kind have you decided on this morning?"

Annie looked at me to see if I was teasing. I wasn't. Dad was looking straight ahead, wearing his "Captain" look, but a smile tugged at the corners of his mouth.

"This morning, I'm leaning toward a Tennessee Walking Horse, but I'd settle for a nice little Morgan or Arab. I think I'll just have to let my heart pick him out. I'll know him when I see him."

All the way to the fairgrounds, she talked about breeds and sizes, colors and markings, training and temperament. Annie had decided, after moving to Pine Hill, that she wanted a mare or a gelding, because stallions generally are not as companionable on rides with groups, and she wanted to be a part of the group rides that her school friends took on most weekends. She was going to look for a comfortable horse, sleek and perky, affectionate and gentle. A horse she wouldn't have to fight every inch of the way. She wanted a friend who would go because he liked to go and because he liked her.

Of course, if he happened to be black with white stockings and a white star, that would be *great*. The Absolutely Perfect Horse. Dad and I had heard the whole tale many times before, but it helped to pass the time.

The Horse Fair was an annual event in Pine Hill. It was the big event of the community. Horsemen came from as far away as Mexico, Canada, California, and Tennessee to show and sell their horses. The horse show that ran at the same time gave them a chance to show their animals' paces and talents. As well as entertaining all comers, it helped to raise the prices of the best animals.

There were classes for all kinds of show horses, performance classes for the working breeds, and halter and equitation classes for children. But the big drawing card was the auction in the afternoon of the final day. There were a lot of horse shows around the country, but very few auctions like this one were held.

Some of the mounts to be sold were prizewinners that would sell for unbelievable prices. I couldn't understand, myself, why anybody would spend more than a thousand dollars on a horse. But fortunately for Annie, there were also ordinary horses for ordinary people at ordinary prices.

4

The parking lot at the fairgrounds was dusty. Cars and pickups, most of them pulling one-, two-, or even four-horse trailers, were gradually melding into featureless lumps, under a coating of the iron-red dust. The work T.C. and I had done in washing and polishing the truck and trailer was going to be wasted. From the scummy look of most of the trailers, nobody else had bothered. Not one seemed to have started the morning as clean as our trailer, or lined at the bottom with fresh hay for the new occupant.

Performance classes were still going on, but Annie said she'd seen enough of that last night at the show. "Let's go down to the barns," she said. "Maybe we can see the horses that are already tagged for sale."

From the looks of the crowds around the barns, a lot of other people had had the same idea. Annie looked at the milling people and pulled Dad toward a shadowy corner of the barn.

"Would you hold this for me, Daddy?" she asked, handing him the leather pouch that held her money.

"You sure?" he asked, hefting it.

"I'd feel better," she answered. "Some of the characters I see around here look pretty raunchy."

He nodded. "O.K., honey. Anybody snatches my purse will get fallen on. Heavily." He tied the strings together and slipped the loop over his belt; then he tucked the pouch under shirt and belt, pulling it around so that the slight bulge didn't show.

"That ought to be safe," he said. "You bring the whole wad?"

"No. One seventy-five. The rest is for feed and stuff."

I forgot about being invisible and snorted, "You won't get a prize Arab with that!"

Dad squelched me with a raised eyebrow. "We should get a pretty fair country riding horse for that," he said calmly.

Annie smiled at him, ignored me, and started down the long, dark corridor of the horse barn. Invisible was better. I dropped a few paces back, but Dad waited for me to catch up.

"Look, this is Annie's day, pal. Don't forget it again, see?" He did a swell Edward G. Robinson, but Little Caesar wouldn't have shaken a guy affectionately by the back of the neck and mussed his hair.

"I see."

As I walked along the stalls slowly, it was easy to match Dad, stride for stride. When he got into a hurry, forget it. Even with his bad leg, I couldn't keep up with him then.

Annie stopped to look at a four-year-old Morgan bay, who seemed nervous, tossing his head and gnawing at the boards on his stall. "That's a bad habit," she observed.

Dad pointed out a nice-sized pinto with a roached mane. "He looks likely."

"Look at his front legs. They both come out of the same sprocket-hole. I'd like a little more brisket," Annie decided, after walking around him for the fifth time.

The sorrel gelding had a milky cast in one eye, and the big roan was Roman nosed and, as his handler finally admitted, hard mouthed.

"Gee, Daddy, none of the horses in my price range are anything like I'm looking for, except maybe the gray Arab." Annie sounded disappointed.

The gray was pretty, even to me. He was five, a good age, and he bowed his neck and lipped carrot slices daintily out of Annie's hand. He had small ears that almost touched at their points, so steep was their arch, when he looked at something with interest.

"We hope to get five hundred for him," his owner said. And that wasn't even a prize horse.

"We're all hot and thirsty. Let's get a cool drink and set a spell, as the natives say, before the auction starts," said Dad, seeing her disappointment.

I agreed, fanning myself with some straw for emphasis. "Those poor horses in the show ring must be dying from the heat," I said. "It's awfully hot for May."

"O.K.," Annie said, agreeable for once. "I saw a booth down there about two barns away." She pointed with her chin. But she didn't have to point; we found the booth by the smell of barbecue cooking on the open grills.

"Is it too early for a sandwich?" I asked Dad.

"Not too early for me," he said and looked at Annie. "How about you?"

"Not too early for me, either. I can't even remember eating breakfast."

A dusty-looking man sat beside me and ordered a sandwich. "You folks come far?" he asked Dad.

"No. Not too far," Dad said. "We're the Braedens. Have a farm out of town about ten miles."

The man nodded and held his hand out to Dad across me, almost knocking my sandwich out of my hand. "I'm Tom Blackburn. Heard about you folks moving onto the old Johnson place. Raising cattle, ain't you? Going in for horses, too, or just looking around?"

"I'm Sam Braeden. These are my children, Pete and Annie," Dad said. "We came to buy Annie a horse."

"But we haven't seen anything I like. At least not anything I can afford," she said.

"What kind of horse you looking for?" he asked.

"A nice riding horse," she said. "But everything

seems to be show horses. Not just horses for people to ride for fun."

"Yeah," he agreed. "I'm looking for a good woods horse myself. Something with good shoulders and enough heart to jump logs and gullies. I raise coon dogs. Sometimes the only way to follow them is on horseback."

"Have you been through all the barns?" Annie asked.

"No. Some of 'em. But don't be discouraged if you don't see just what you're looking for in the barns. All the sale horses aren't in those stalls. Some are still in trailers. There are probably quite a few that won't be tagged until this afternoon. And besides"— he smiled—"bid what you can afford to pay on any horse that takes your fancy. You never can tell. You might get a bargain. A real bargain. It has happened."

Mr. Blackburn slid off his stool, his sandwich finished. "See you folks around."

After he was gone, Annie seemed more cheerful. Probably dreaming about maybe owning that pretty gray Arab.

"If the horses won't even be tagged until this afternoon, let's go look at the sideshow," I said. I was tired of looking at horses.

The big carnival was as much a part of the horse fair as the horses. The kids at school talked a lot about the shows from previous years. There had been twin dog-faced boys, a man who ate light bulbs and razor blades, a fat lady with a red beard, magic shows, and one tent kids didn't get into where ladies took off their clothes to music.

We played some of the gyp games that Dad called "ponies" and ate popcorn while we worked our way down the midway toward a long tent that stood apart from the others.

INDIAN MUSEUM, its banner proclaimed. GENUINE ARTIFACTS OF THE EARLY WEST. INDIAN MUMMY. Original costume worn by CHIEF CRAZY HORSE at LITTLE BIG HORN MASSACRE. GENUINE GENERAL CUSTER'S GENUINE SADDLE. SEE THE NECKLACE made of the KNUCKLEBONES OF CUSTER'S TROOPERS. THOUSANDS OF GENUINE ARTICLES of the *EARLY WEST.*

"Can we go into this one, Daddy? It looks pretty good." It was the first interest Annie had shown since we left the barns.

"I can hardly wait to see Custer's saddle," Dad said, very wryly. "It must have had a nail in it pointing the wrong way, or the old boy wouldn't have been so proddy."

The only museum that would interest my dad was one about ships and Navy stuff, but he paid the tired-looking man at the front entrance.

As the tall guy handed out the mimeographed guidebooks, I looked him over. He was the tallest man I had ever seen. Dad was over six feet by a couple of inches or so, but this guy was at least a head taller. Only he kind of slumped over and let his shoulders round off, something my dad would never do. *He* was as straight as a mainmast.

The tall man had a black-and-white badge pinned on his shirt. It said WALKER, and I guessed that was his name. He seemed uninterested in us until Annie walked past him. He reached out and touched one of her pony tails with a not-too-clean finger.

"Say," he said. "I just lost my Indian Maiden. Don't suppose you'd be interested?"

Annie and I both looked at Dad, whose eyebrows were climbing.

The tall man saw the expression too and muttered, "No. I suppose not," to answer his own question.

"But thank you very much for asking me," Annie said. "Nobody ever thought I looked like an Indian Maiden before." Annie's not always too smart, but she *is* polite.

"You look more genuine than most of my artifacts," the man said, nodding toward the tent. "And a whole heap better than the Indian pony the Maiden is supposed to ride."

Annie's face fell, and I must have showed my disappointment too, because Walker hastened to add, "Oh, they're genuine enough. But old, real old. They've been carried around a lot, and that wears on an exhibit real bad."

"Custer's saddle, too?" Dad asked. From his tone, I knew he didn't think it really was Custer's saddle.

"Well"—the man scratched his head, judging us shrewdly with his pale eyes to see how much we could be expected to swallow. "It was bought in South Da-

34

kota from a man who swore he got it off the Indian who took it from Custer's dead horse. Nobody could be positive. Them Indians lie a lot. But it's fancier than most. Not issue McClellan, for sure. Got his monogram burned into the leather. It's most likely his saddle, all right."

Dad didn't say anything but took each of us by the arm and walked us into the tent. The man called after us with a weary note in his voice, "Let me know how you like the exhibit."

"A tourist trap, Daddy?" Annie asked. We had learned long ago about those crummy "museums" that line the highways of the far west. Very few of them have anything worth the price of admisssion. Mostly they are full of cheap plastic "souvenirs" that have nothing to do with the location they're supposed to remind you of and are just the same cheap things you saw in the last museum, with a different decal stuck on. Even I had outgrown that junk.

"Maybe. Maybe not. We'll see," Dad said.

5

It was and it wasn't. Most of the things in the illuminated glass cases looked dusty. The mummy looked even drier than a mummy ought to look. Many of the arrowheads in the cases had slipped out of their positions on the glued-down patterns and lay in the bottom, helter-skelter.

The beaded buckskins marked CRAZY HORSE BATTLE DRESS were much more elaborate than any of my reading would lead me to think that a chief would wear into battle.

"I always thought Indians went into battle pretty near naked," I said.

"So did I," Dad agreed.

The most interesting thing, to me, was the necklace

made out of finger bones, supposedly from the trigger fingers of Custer's men. It was gruesome. The bones were drilled through the top and hung down the long way. In between the longer finger bones were some small grayish beads or bones, round ones. There were more than thirty finger bones, but Annie pulled me away from the case before I finished counting.

Maybe this would be a good place to explain about me. I like to count things. I don't know why, I just do it. I count cows in the fields as we drive along. I count fence posts, telephone poles between towns, rosebuds on the new bushes in Mom's flower beds. I knew to the dot how many holes were in the ceiling tiles of my classroom and how many ceiling tiles were in the school building. I knew how many light bulbs were in the fixtures in the church, how many bricks were in the chimney at home.

I like to count things because numbers are definite and solid, and I like good hard facts. Not many people go for that explanation, though, and Annie usually would get exasperated with me when she wanted to move on and I stood there counting something.

"Come on, Petey. Look at the saddles," she said. "There must be two hundred of them."

There weren't two hundred. There were only ninety-three, not counting Custer's, which was in a case by itself. It was fancy, all right. Too fancy. It looked more like pictures of the gear used by Spanish hidalgos. It had those fancy leather covers over the stirrups, and silver, lots of silver, all over it.

The rest of the saddles were behind a single strand

of rope. They sat on wooden frames, and every kind of saddle I had ever seen pictures of or read about seemed to be there. There were some I never imagined. Regular-issue McClellans, sidesaddles of many kinds, early Spanish ones with rusting iron stirrups and high backs. Cowboy saddles so high in front and back that it was easy to see how a man could ride for days on a cattle drive and sleep on his moving horse.

There were pack saddles, English flat saddles, early American saddles without horns, right on up to the modern calf ropers that aren't much but horn and stirrups. The rich, oiled-leather smell was a contrast to the dankness of the exhibit cases.

The saddles ended at the exit door, and the sunlight outside was so bright that for a moment we just stood blinking, trying to regain our vision. Annie got hers back first, or maybe it was instinct that took her to the little corral just outside the exit.

"Look. It's the genuine Indian pony," she said.

"How many Indians do you know who plow?" Dad asked her.

Annie looked at the horse seriously, as she did at all horses. "I don't think he's a plow horse. See, he has old saddle galls on his back and belly, but no harness marks anywhere. On an old fellow like him that would show."

Something did show. He was old, a real nag. His striped hooves were huge and cracked. The only shoe he had on was loose, and it clacked when he walked over to the fence to beg for sugar. His knees were knobby-looking, with bald patches. The upper legs were chunky, and the shoulders and hips seemed flat and kind of hollowed out where they should have been fat. The backbone was pretty straight, but it was sharp, and his ribs were easy to count. His neck was hollow, too, and seemed almost too skinny to hold up his head. Still, the head itself was reasonably good-looking.

For one thing, he looked smart. He had small, cleanly shaped ears that would have been nice if he had held them up instead of letting them flop tiredly in different directions. The eyes were nice, too, dark and clear, with no white showing in the eye, just a small outline around it.

His nose wasn't runny like those of some of the horses we'd looked at, but his large nostrils were just about as funny-looking. I didn't like the way his lower lip hung loose under his chin, either.

"It gives him a sad, hopeless expression," I said.

He was dusty, like everything else at the fair-grounds, but beneath the dust was a faded brownish color with big white spots on his behind. His mane and tail were turning gray from their original color. The were still long and silky-looking, though. Old, yeah, but pretty nice-looking, all in all.

Annie gave me a couple of carrot slices, and I held them out to him. He pushed them around my palm with velvet-covered lips and dropped them in the dirt.

"I don't think he has enough teeth to chew with."

"He likes us," Annie said, reaching through the fence to scratch behind his ears. The old horse sighed noisily and moved closer to the fence so she could reach him better.

"I don't think he can chew carrots," I said again. "Don't you have any sugar?"

Annie brought sugar from another pocket, and the old horse lifted the cubes carefully from her hand. None of them dropped to the ground.

"At his age," she said, "I don't suppose it matters that sugar isn't good for his teeth."

"No teeth," Dad said. "Good thing, too. You guys are going to put out your hands to a strange horse one day, and draw back bloody stumps."

"Oh, no. Not this fellow," Annie crooned in the voice she reserved for the baby and assorted visiting children.

Dad waited patiently, as we patted the old horse. "Don't you think we'd better get a seat? It's twelve-thirty. Auction ought to be starting soon, Annie," he finally said, when he was tired of waiting.

From behind us at the exit door of the tent the tall man said, "He's a friendly old cayuse. I'm going to miss him, in a way."

Annie, who had just about caught up with Dad and me, stopped and turned back. Dad sighed and stopped, shifting from foot to foot wearily. His leg hurt when he stood too long.

"Is he the Indian Maiden's horse?" she asked.

Walker laughed. "The Indian Maiden never saw a horse until she came to work for me. She wouldn't even feed the old Chief here if I didn't make her do it. Reckon he's one of the reasons she took off."

"If she's not taking him, why are you going to miss him?" Annie asked persistently.

"Look at him. I need a more likely-looking horse. What better place to get one than at an auction? I saw a little pinto over there, ought to go cheap. He won't be much of a using horse, but he's flashy and that's what I need."

"What are you going to do with *him*?" Annie sounded suspicious. "Sell him at the auction?"

Walker laughed again. "Why, missy, they'd plumb laugh me out of the arena. No, I called some people I know to come pick him up. He's no good for anything but dogmeat anymore."

Annie gasped and turned to Dad. She didn't say anything out loud. She didn't have to.

"Now, Annie. We're just a one-horse farm. Not a home for worn-out Indian ponies." He turned to Walker. "If you'd feed him once in a while, maybe he wouldn't be so worn out."

The tall man sighed. "It ain't that, mister. Don't get huffy. I treat him good. He didn't never eat elegant, but neither do I. He eats plenty, he's just plain old. I got papers that show he's coming nigh onto thirty-five. I got to have a horse with a little spunk. Something to catch the kiddies' eyes when the Indian Maiden rides him down the midway."

Annie reached out and put her hand on Dad's arm, but she was talking to Walker. "How much do the dogmeat people pay?"

"One horse, Annie," Dad said. "One horse is all we have room for, and one horse is all we are going to get. This old fellow is dead on his feet. Come on, let's go to the auction."

"I don't want to go to the auction, Daddy. This is the horse I want."

I was too stunned to snicker. This old beat-up bundle of bones was as far from the A.P.H. we had heard so much about as it was possible to get.

"No, missy," the tall man said, sounding concerned. "You get on over to the auction with your dad. A pretty little lady like you needs a perky little horse to ride. You couldn't never ride this old fellow. Why, his heart nearly pounds out of his chest when he walks from the corral to the trailer. He ain't no horse for you."

I walked back to Annie and tugged her arm. "Come on, Annie . . . the auction'll be starting. You might miss a chance at a good horse."

She didn't answer me, just gently lifted her arm away from my hand. Annie was so much like Mom sometimes, it was spooky. She had that strange set look Mom gets sometimes when she's determined to do something and is just a little scared it might not be the right thing. Dad called it Mom's Irish streak . . . "*Mad* Irish streak" was the way he actually put it.

I noticed that he'd seen Annie's expresson, too, and I tried again. "Annie, that's been a good old horse, but he's sure not the A.P.H. Let's go look at that gray Arab again. Maybe he'll go for just what you want to pay.

She turned back to Walker and said, "How much?"

"Never you mind," the tall man's voice was sharp now. "He ain't for sale to you. I done called the dogmeat people. You go on over to the auction and get your Ayrab. I might even see you over there after the truck comes. I got to get me another Indian pony."

Annie ignored me, looked at Dad. "Daddy, I know I can't have another horse. You said I could have any horse I could afford. I want this one."

Dad threw up his hands in defeat. "Little-Mother-of-the-World wants the horse," he said to Walker. "How much?"

6

Walker looked at both of them. He thought they were crazy, I could tell. He didn't include me in his look because he could see I was on his side. In Dad's shoes, I'd have dragged the girl away from there kicking and screaming, if I'd had to, after all we'd heard about the Absolutely Perfect Horse. For some reason of his own, Dad had decided to let her make her own decision, however dumb it might be.

"Man, I don't like to tell you," Walker said. "They give me what he's worth in dogmeat. Twenty-five dollars. But he's not worth that as a keeping horse."

Dad pulled the pouch from under his shirt and belt and peeled off a twenty and a five. "Make out a bill of sale while I get the trailer," he said, turning on his heel and striding off. The set of his shoulders made me feel small and empty inside.

Now that it was done, Annie looked scared. She climbed inside the corral with the old horse and put her arm over his neck.

Walker looked at me and shook his head, looking from me to the money in his hand, to the girl and the horse. "Takes all kinds," he said at last and disappeared into the tent to get the bill of sale.

I climbed onto the fence and hung my arms over the top rail. "Annie . . ."

"I don't want to talk about it, Petey," she said.

She stood, rubbing the horse's forehead with her left hand and the soft spot under his jaws with her right. The old nag leaned against her with his eyes half closed. If he'd been a cat, he'd have purred.

From the tent came the sound of laughter and voices, as a group of visitors drifted out into the sunshine. I didn't have to see them to know that one of them was Cathy Thompson. She wasn't one of Annie's friends . . . or anybody else's. She was always in the middle of any group of people, her high-pitched, supersweet voice soaring above all the others. She was the high school bulletin board. Annie looked kind of sick.

"Well, well. Look who's tending the livestock. Hi, Annie. Who's your friend?"

"Hello, Cathy." I thought Annie used remarkable restraint in her tone. "Meet the Chief."

Cathy sniffed. "Chief? That's the genuine Indian pony? Looks more like the sole survivor of the Custer

Massacre." She pronounced the last word mas-sa-CREE, with a contemptuous twang. Two others in the group laughed. Ross Blackburn was wrapped around Cathy like a vine around a tree, and Tanya Bale, the Genuine Beauty Queen, was just behind them. But the slender, dark-haired boy who walked beside Tanya didn't laugh. He glanced at his friends impatiently and smiled at Annie. A nice smile, not a snicker.

When you're just a kid in junior high, the high school kids mostly don't seem to know you're around—or even alive. Tanya and some of Annie's other friends had been to our house several times, but I didn't remember them ever saying so much as hello to me. Evan Christophoulis was different.

From the first time he had delivered the groceries from his father's store to our house and discovered that T.C. was Vietnamese, a foreigner, they'd been friends. Perhaps it was because he was a Greek-born naturalized citizen. Or maybe he was just friendly. Anyway, he took T.C. as his special project. He took him places: movies and ball games; worked out on the farm with us when his father could spare him at the store; tutored T.C. when school started, in the subjects that were hard for him. English and history, mainly. T.C. didn't need any tutoring in math and science. He could hold his own there.

I liked Evan. He treated me as if I were a real person, not a younger brother. I was almost as tall as he was, standing on the lower rail of the fence. Evan hung his arms over the top rail, too.

"Hi, Petey," he said and nodded toward the Chief. "Seems nice and gentle."

Tanya tugged at him to pull him away from the fence. "Asleep, you mean."

Annie didn't say anything else. Hoping they'd go away, I suspect. She didn't mention that the horse was hers, which wasn't at all strange. A horse like that would take some explaining, and Annie would rather do it herself than have Cathy bray it all over school.

They turned to go, each couple arm in arm, but they had to stop as a stake-bed truck pulled up to the corral, raising clouds of dust. Before the dust even started to settle, an unshaven man in a torn khaki shirt and dirty pants stepped down.

Without his saying a word, I knew this was the dogmeat man. Annie knew it too. She was pale and really frightened-looking. Walker said he had called them, but somehow I never expected to see them. The old horse raised his head and peered forward expectantly. A truck to him meant moving on. He didn't know it would have been his final trip.

"That the horse?" the dirty man asked, and spat tobacco juice expertly over the fence between the animal's front hooves.

Annie stiffened and stood closer to her horse. "No, he's not. I mean he's the horse you came to get, but you can't have him now."

"Look-a-here. I know this seems bad to a kid, but the old nag won't never know the difference. Look at him. I'm doin' him a favor."

47

The man was opening the corral gate and moving inside as he spoke. He took hold of the halter. "Just move away now, and I'll get him loaded."

Without turning my head, I knew that Evan had come back and was standing beside me at the fence, not saying a word. It was like one of those nightmares when everything moves in slow motion. Annie moved as if her body were encased in cold honey. Even her speech seem slower.

"You can't take him," she said.

The man started to push her away and lead the old horse out of the corral. I was aware that Evan was no longer beside me, but in the corral behind Annie.

"I wouldn't," he said.

The trucker stared. Evan's move had been so easy and quiet that it occurred before anyone knew it was happening. Now Evan stood there, just behind Annie, balanced on the balls of his feet, flipping an empty Coke bottle up into the air and catching it by the neck, as it came down. The action was both graceful and strangely menacing.

"You keep out of this, kid," the trucker said, angry, now. "I was called to come git this nag, and I'm gonna git him." He reached again for the halter he had dropped when Evan vaulted the fence. Annie had hold of it now, and she wasn't about to let it go. I could see our pickup coming and I knew she could, too.

"Ease off, friend," Evan said, still flipping the Coke bottle and not raising his voice a hair. "The little lady doesn't want you to lay hands on her horse."

The trucker made a "come here" motion at the cab of the truck. A man who had been sitting slumped in the front seat unfolded from the right-hand side and slammed the door loudly as he came around the front of the cab.

"You havin' trouble, Frank?" he asked in a growly voice. There was an air of violence about him that made me shiver. He was big, a head and shoulders taller than Evan.

But if his size worried Evan, Evan didn't let it show. He continued to smile a gentle half smile, and the Coke bottle never missed a flip. Ross came over to the corral and began to climb the fence slowly. Cathy tugged at him, saying, "Keep out of this. That old nag isn't worth fighting about."

The trucker nodded in her direction. "Listen to your friend, there. This old horse is nearly gone. It'll be a mercy to let me take him. Now don't you two give me any more trouble. I'll just take that horse and be on my way."

"I've already bought him. You can't have him," Annie said. "Just because he's old, he's not useless."

"He ain't useless at all." The trucker grinned at her. "He'll make good dogmeat. That's useful." Then his smile faded, and his eyes narrowed. "What do you mean, you've already bought him?"

When the trucker had laughed about dogmeat being useful, Evan's smile froze. The bottle stopped flipping. He just held it loosely by its neck.

"She's bought the horse, friend. She isn't going to sell it to you. Now get out of the corral." He didn't raise his voice, but I was shivering just the same and hanging on to the fence tightly, wishing Dad would hurry.

"Look, kid. We don't want trouble, but we came thirty miles out here to pick up this dogmeat, and I done told you two or three times. We're goin' to git him."

The big man was beside the trucker, now. Behind them, Dad stopped the pickup beside their truck. I didn't see him step down, but there was no mistaking his voice when it cracked across the corral like a whip. "What's the trouble, Annie?"

"This is the dogmeat man, Daddy. He won't believe that I've bought the horse."

The two men turned when Dad spoke. As they parted, I could see that he was poised just inside the gate. I'd never seen him look like this. His shoulders were squared and slightly forward, and his feet were evenly placed, but slightly apart, as if he were ready to jump forward or to either side. He gave the impression of being crouched to fight. From his expression, I thought he might welcome a chance to swing at somebody.

Evan began the slow flip, flip of the Coke bottle again. The grin returned to his lips. The odds had evened up.

"Mister, you'd better believe it," Dad said, in that tone that officers and schoolteachers develop early in their careers, if they are to be successful. "I don't know what my daughter sees in that old horse, but she wants him, and she's paid for him. Take your argument up with the man who used to own him."

The trucker and his partner looked at each other and shuffled their feet, uncertain, now, of their position. "Look, I don't know anything but what I'm told. Walker called on the phone and said to come get the horse. I pay good money, and I had a long trip out here. I ain't trying to steal the horse."

"Go inside and get Walker, Annie," said Dad.

"Get Walker for what?" The tall man came out of the tent. "Uh-oh!" he said, as his eyes adjusted to the glare, and he took in the situation. "I thought you might get the old Chief away before they got here."

"Well, what did you call *me* for?" The trucker was angry, and he wasn't afraid to show Walker that he was.

"Never occurred to me that somebody might want the old Chief. The little lady wants him. Paid just what you'd have paid. Reckon he's her horse."

The trucker cursed briefly but choked off his outburst when he looked at Dad. He motioned his helper out of the corral, and they waited for Dad to move away from the gate. Neither of them seemed to want to shove past him. When they were both in the truck, Dad turned and watched them until they were out of sight. They clashed their gears as they drove away.

I was shivering, and Annie looked as if she would have fallen down without her firm grip on Chief's mane.

51

"You O.K.?" Dad asked Annie, though his glance included me.

"Sure." She nodded. "Fine, now. I certainly was scared there for a while, though. I thought he was going to take the horse in spite of anything I said."

"Hey, evzone," Dad said, holding out his hand to Evan. "Thanks for stepping in."

Evan flipped the Coke bottle to his left hand. He gripped Dad's hand with his right. "T.C. said sometimes you were twelve feet tall. I never saw it before today."

Dad was pleased. He grinned at Evan and said, "Now, now. You know I'm a peaceful man!"

"Yeah," Evan agreed. "Real peaceful."

From across the fence Tanya said, "Evan, come on!"

"Yes, come on. Evan, Ross! We've still got a lot of things to see and do this afternoon," Cathy called.

And tell, I thought.

"Thank you, Evan," Annie said.

He just smiled at us, as if nothing had happened and we were passing in the hall at school. Then he put his hands on top of the fence and vaulted it again, light as a feather. He ran a hand over my hair, standing it on end, as he turned away. "I thought you were in a hurry," he said to Tanya. "Let's stop by the Coke stand. I'd like to drop off this empty and get another. It's a very warm day."

7

I climbed down from the fence and let down the tail-gate of the trailer. Then I went into the gate to stand beside Dad. He was talking with Walker. Although the whiplash was gone out of his voice, I could tell he was still annoyed . . . as much at himself as at anyone.

"You said you'd called them. It just didn't soak into me that you'd committed the horse to them."

"I thought you'd be gone with the Chief before they got here. . . . I'm sorry about the trouble, Mr. Braeden. Old Chief's been with me a long time. Guess I wanted you folks to have him, instead of them, even if he ain't good for much."

"He'll be all right," Annie told him. "I'll take very good care of him."

"He ain't sick, missy," Walker said. "Just old and wore out. I doubt there's much you can do to build him up, but I'm glad he's going to a good home. He deserves it."

Annie lifted the old horse's head, almost holding it up by main strength with the worn halter he was wearing. She started leading him to the trailer. Walker stopped her. "Here," he said. "I reckon he's earned these things. He's wore 'em long enough."

He pulled a beaded bridle with a straight snaffle bit from its peg on the fence and handed it to Annie. Then he took the light Indian-design blanket and fastened it around the Chief with a wide surcingle, which had little stirrups attached. The old horse held his own head up once the gear was on; he thought, perhaps, that it was time for the show. He didn't even know that the big show had already taken place.

"A few Indian Maidens back, we used to rope off him some. He was real flashy then, but past his prime for cow work. He had some good years in the rodeo, I'm told. We had to quit roping with him, though. His legs just gave out on him. About a hundred yards is all he's good for, missy. I hope you won't be sorry you got him."

Walker helped Annie mount. "Ride him around a bit, then he'll think the show's over. He'll go right into the trailer. He's a good traveler. Had lots of practice."

Annie looked good on the horse, and he looked

better, too. While he was being ridden he didn't look so dopey. He lifted his big feet high and gave his head little tosses, like an actor trying to hog attention. I wondered if the saddle blanket was enough to pad away the sharpness of his backbone and ribs. When he shifted leads, I could see the muscles pull along his thin shoulders and hips.

Annie rode slowly around the corral several times before she nodded to me. I pushed the gate open, and she rode him into the trailer. I thought that was dumb, but it turned out to be safe enough. The old horse was trailer wise. He stood still, without breathing, until he felt Annie catch hold of the high side and pull herself off his back. Then he heaved a tremendous noisy sigh and relaxed, cock hipped, his head drooping almost to the hay-covered floor.

He was the picture of someone who has done a hard day's work and needs a long sleep to recover from it. Annie pulled his head up long enough to substitute the halter she had brought for the new horse, in place of the beaded bridle. She hung that on a peg, strapping it down with the chap strap that was there for the purpose. In an open trailer, gear can fly out if it's not carefully attached. Especially when it's light stuff.

While Annie rode, I listened to Walker tell Dad about the old Chief. He really was an Indian pony, born in the herd at the Blackfoot reservation in Montana. He had been trained for calf roping by a Blackfoot boy who wanted to follow the rodeo circuit. The colt had been smart and flashy and big enough to throw the heaviest calf. Finally, when the offers of big money for the horse got to be too much for the boy, who wasn't doing well as a rodeo performer, he sold him. The horse went through a series of owners, some good ropers, some poor ones, until he was too old for the arena.

Walker had been with a little carnival at the Chief's last rodeo, and he heard he was going to be sold for very little. He bought the horse, worked him easy, made a kind of pet out of him. The animal was affectionate and liked children. When the Indian Maiden rode him down the midway, all dressed up in her buckskins, they usually drew a good crowd back to the exhibit.

Dad shook hands with Walker when he was sure Annie had the loading completed.

"I'll take good care of him, Mr. Walker. He'll have a good home," Annie called again from the pickup.

"I know you will, missy. Thank you," Walker called back as we slowly pulled toward the road.

I stuck my head out of the window and waved. He waved back. The tall man stood there until the dust and a curve in the road put him out of my sight. The last I saw of him he looked more bent over than usual . . . bent and very sad.

There wasn't much to say. Annie had a horse. About as far from the A.P.H. we had started out to buy as it was possible to be. What had come over Annie to make her insist on that poor bony creature in the trailer behind us I would never figure. One thing I knew for sure. Anything I said would be wrong, so

I managed to keep quiet while four or five hundred questions marched around inside my head.

Dad broke the silence, after a bit, by clearing his throat and saying, "Well, Annie. You've got your horse."

"Daddy, when Dr. Kurt comes over to get his trailer this evening, I'll talk to him. He can tell me what to feed the Chief, how to take care of him."

"Annie," said Dad in a very gentle voice, "I talked with Mr. Walker while you were riding. The horse is at least thirty-five years old. Probably more. That's about a hundred and fifty years for a person. Horses and people just don't ordinarily live that long. I think you'd better realize for now and always that he isn't going to get well. He isn't sick. Just old."

Annie stared at her hands that she was holding between her dusty knees. "I guess I really understand that, Daddy."

"If you want to, I think Dr. Kurt could find someone with some small children who want a pet more than a riding horse. Someone who would get a kick out of owning a genuine Indian pony . . . and who would give him a good home. Then we could find you a riding horse."

Annie seemed to think that over. From her expression, I knew what the answer would be. "No, Daddy. I looked at the horses that were up for sale at the auction, and none of them was what I wanted. But when we walked out of that tent, and I saw the Chief, I wanted him. Old and bedraggled as he is. He is the horse I wanted."

"The Absolutely Perfect Horse," I said.

Annie looked over at me. She wasn't even angry. "Are you very disappointed, Petey?"

A dumb question. Of course I was disappointed. I mean, having a real Indian pony is all right, if he is an Indian pony you can ride and be proud of. But a *retired* Indian pony? I'd rather have had the pinto with the funny front legs. At least he could have been ridden.

"It wasn't my choice," I said.

Dad nodded. "That's right, Petey. Not your choice. If Annie's satisfied, that's all that matters."

"What's Mom going to say? And T.C.?" I asked.

"It's not what Mom is going to say that worries me." Annie ignored anything T.C. might possibly think. "It's what Cathy Thompson is going to spread all over school by Monday morning."

"You're going to be kidded," I said. "You talked too much about the wonderful horse you were going to buy."

"Keep your chin up, my little chickadee," Dad said. "You've taken a big bite. Now it's up to you to chew it."

"Yeah," Annie said. She leaned her face on her arms, which were now stretched out and braced against the dash.

We were out on the main highway now, and Dad's attention was on the road. Annie didn't want to talk anymore, so I stared out the window and wondered what had happened to my only sister. She never used to be a dumb dope. Oh, once in a while she'd do dopey things. What girl didn't? But this was a dumb stunt to top everything crazy she had ever done.

If we had just not gone to the carnival! Was it my fault? I was the one who had wanted to see the side-shows. If we had gone to the auction instead, she might have gotten the gray Arab. Even that fence-chewing bay would have been better than no riding horse at all.

Instead, Annie had let her feelings get mixed up in it, and now she had no horse, but a pet. A liability. She had talked about a companion, but she had bought a patient. Thank goodness, he hadn't cost much . . . though I was afraid the rest of her money might well be spent on vet's fees, trying to get him into shape for riding.

Still, there was something about the old horse. He had carried Indian Maidens down the midway, doing their little act for children, all across the country. Nearly forty years old. Dad was about that age. Forty horse-years equal a hundred and fifty people-years. No wonder he shuffled and dragged his feet when he walked.

Funny, though, how he came to life when Walker put the gear on him and Annie mounted. He perked right up and tried to do his act. There was pride in that . . . he did try. Dad always said the best anybody could do was to try.

The truck slowed, and we turned carefully into the road that led to our farm. "Land ho!" Dad said, as the house came into sight.

"Batten down the hatches . . . shore up all lines!

We're about to hit a squall, mytes. Lubbers below!"
I had a pretty good pirate voice, if I do say so myself.

What it was wasn't exactly a squall. More like the eye of a hurricane. The shocked silence that greeted the Chief when he backed from the trailer with his bony lack of grace, then stood in an attitude of utter weariness, was just what I'd read about, in the center of such a storm. Mom didn't criticize him. The look she gave Dad, though, was something to see.

Annie talked too much, too fast, as she introduced the Chief to Mom and told about buying him away from the dogmeat men. That was a bomb. She should have saved that part for later, when Mom was more used to the sight of him. Everything had to be explained by Dad (and me, too), but no amount of explanation erased the creases from between Mom's eyebrows.

The only unqualified approval the Chief got came from Brad. He liked anything or anyone big. The bigger the better. He always held his arms out to the tallest person around. Though he still crawled rather than walked, he would climb anything that had a handhold. It was a constant task to locate him and get him down from whatever high perch he had climbed to.

When Annie backed the horse from the trailer, Brad came out of the yard as fast as his hands and knees would carry him and planted himself in front of the horse. Then he demanded, with upraised arms and loud squeals, to be picked up. The Chief sniffed at the top of his head with velvety nostrils, making Brad crow with delight. Annie picked the baby up and swung him onto the Chief's back, where he clung, laughing and yelling, as she walked the horse slowly toward his shed.

"Sam," Mom said, when Annie was beyond hearing, "where on earth did she ever see that thing? How could you let her buy that?"

"It's the horse she wanted. For some reason, he's special to her. We'll just have to let her work it out. I could no more have stopped her than I could stop you from doing something you're set on doing. You know how much like you she is."

Mom saw I was listening, so she didn't say anything else. I had the idea that the end of the subject hadn't been explored, as far as she was concerned.

Still, I had a warm feeling from Dad's answer. He didn't know any better than I did why Annie had chosen the horse. I don't think there was a reason. Annie probably couldn't explain it to herself. But the good feeling came when I realized that Dad would go along with her judgment and was willing to let her make her own mistakes, as he would someday allow me to make mine. He would help where he could.

I followed Annie and Brad out to the shed that Dad, T.C., and I had built for the horse. It was built in the old-timey way, out of rough pine logs cut from the young trees we had cleared from our pasture. It was closed to the north, east, and west, open to the south. The roof extended several feet past the closed part of the shed to provide cool shade. Everything roof was floored deeply with sand and native m the creek bed, covered over with straw. morning, someone had sprinkled fresh, sweet-ferns from the woods and yellow field daisies all over the straw floor. There were bunches of yellow brown-eyed Susans in the corners of the feed trough, which was filled with fresh grain. In the center of the grain were three carrots, with the tops still on, standing upright, like birthday candles.

Not someone. Taro Chan. I never knew a boy to like flowers the way he did. As each new sort of flower bloomed in the fields and the woods, he came in carrying one carefully selected blossom to show Mom and to compare with the pictures in the books we had. He'd even go to the library to find one that we couldn't identify at home. In the months we had been on the farm, I guess he had learned more about the flowers in this part of the country than most of the natives knew. Latin names, too!

The Chief paid more attention to the flowers than Annie did. He sniffed at the brown-eyed Susans in the feed bin, but he decided they weren't as good to eat as the grain. He buried his nose in that and began to grind with his jaws.

"I think he's going to have to have bran, or something like that, instead of grain," Annie said. "His teeth are about gone."

"After you waited such a long time . . . I mean, you've wanted a horse ever since I can remember . . . why would you pick a toothless old nag? He really isn't good for anything but dogmeat."

I thought she was going to clobber me with the currycomb. "Don't you say that. Don't ever say that."

"It's true. I mean, he's nice and all that, but you can't ride him with your friends."

"That isn't everything."

"I knew that all along," I said, pushing my luck.

"I didn't know you knew it."

Annie went on currying the Chief's mane, a little harder than necessary. The horse didn't seem to mind, though.

"Well, Petey," she said, finally, "I've been thinking about it too. I guess when the time comes to choose, you have to go where your heart goes and forget the plans and the fancy dreams. There was just something about him. I couldn't let him go like that. It just wasn't right."

I took the rough cloth she had for rubbing him down and began to polish the dust off his neck and front quarters. "You sound like something Dad said to us."

"When?" she asked suspiciously.

"When you felt so bad about his bringing Taro Chan home with him."

Annie didn't look at me. She disengaged Brad's grip on the mane close to the saddle-pad, so she could curry that too. Then she was occupied with soothing the baby's indignant wails until she finished and let him grab the mane again.

"I really don't see any connection at all," she said, at last.

"Why don't you like T.C., Annie? He likes you."

63

"Why wouldn't he?" she asked in that sharp tone she always used when T.C. was the subject. "He loves me from the teeth out."

"That's not true!" I was getting angry again. The dust was flying off the Chief's rump in clouds that made me sneeze. It's hard to sound mad while you're sneezing.

Annie caught hold of my shirt and pulled me out into the fresh air. "Here. Breathe for a minute, before you get your allergies all stirred up. Don't tell me you're going to be allergic to horses, too."

"I think it's the dust," I said, between sneezes.

The baby wobbled and almost fell. Annie flew back into the shed and took him down. She brought him outside and set him on top of the rough pine-log fence that ran along the east side of the shelter. She steadied him with one hand, trying to keep his hands out of her hair with the other.

"Petey, Taro Chan is not our real brother. I wish you'd remember that. I know you're crazy about him, and that's O.K. Just don't ask me to be."

"But why, Annie?" I couldn't understand her at all. "He tries so hard. It just isn't like you to dislike anybody."

"If you'd really listen to some of those tales Daddy tells, really listen, you'd know why. He's nothing but an Oriental opportunist. He shifted from one side to the other, until he got into the river patrol and began attaching himself to our naval unit. When he found our daddy, a good soft touch, he dug in like a seed tick."

"That's not fair!" I declared. "Did you ever think how it must be for somebody his age to have lost his family so early he can't remember them? Or how much he must have needed someone to be 'family' for him? Besides, you're twisting things around. And he saved Dad's life."

"His own, too. Remember?"

"Everybody at school likes him," I said, shifting tactics.

"Not everyone," Annie said, her voice grim. "And those that do fawn over him until it makes me sick. He's their token Oriental. An escapee from the Communists. It makes my stomach turn."

"Evan doesn't fawn over anybody," I said. I knew instantly that that wasn't a good example, for she didn't particularly like Evan, either . . . at least, she hadn't before today.

"Evan doesn't have to. Everybody chases after him because he's one of those fractional backs on the football team. I don't know what his motive is for letting Taro Chan hang around him, but I'll bet he's got a motive."

"He helps Evan with his math. Evan helps him with history and English. They're lab partners in science. If they weren't both foreign-born, you wouldn't see a thing wrong with that."

"That's something else. I don't see how Taro Chan could be passing all his courses, unless the teachers are just letting him pass. Since they stopped social promotions here, the girls tell me it's a lot harder school than it used to be."

"And that's not fair, either. That's not even rational. You know T.C. went to school in Thailand. From what Dad tells me, those Catholic schools are tough. He took all kinds of tests before they made out his schedule at school. Dad says he's got a terrific I.Q."

"Dad says." Annie sounded bitter and looked unhappy.

I had a sudden flash of insight. "I don't think you're thinking for yourself, anymore. You don't sound like *you*. I think you're listening to Tanya and that bunch. They're pretty dumb, even for girls. If you ask me, they're a sorry bunch to take for friends."

"I didn't ask you," Annie said with a sniff. "But since you think you know so much, everyone at school is *not* as fond of T.C. as you are."

My temper was getting out of hand. I gave Annie the cloth I'd been using to polish the Chief's rump and took the baby down from the fence rail. I put him under one arm and started for the house.

"Well, you didn't ask me, but I'll tell you, anyway," I threw back over my shoulder. "You don't talk like my sister, anymore. I'm glad you got old Dogmeat, because you can't ride him with that snotty bunch."

I probably would have said more, but the baby squirmed so that I nearly dropped him. I had to put all my attention to getting him right side up and out of the corral gate. By the time I had explained to Mom that I wasn't killing Brad, it wasn't any use to go into the spat with Annie. Being the middle kid is not always easy. Especially when you have been the youngest for a long time.

66

8

While Mom measured tea leaves into the blue-and-gold teapot nobody was allowed to touch but her, I sat behind the table on my bench. I was thinking about the day and counting the knots in the new pine paneling. The new kitchen was nice. Nicer than the one we'd left behind, actually. It was so big.

Before it had become our kitchen, this room had been the parlor of the old house. It had a fireplace on the outside wall, and that was all that remained of the original structure. Dad had the carpenters enclose the part of the front porch that ran in front of the parlor with glass windows. That was where Mom kept her plants. There were also comfortable chairs with bright cushions and a wicker couch painted pale yellow with green cushions. The dining table was arranged so everyone had a good view from the windows. It was pleasant in the winter months to have the greenery inside. And, as now, in spring and summer we could look beyond the growing things to the outside.

From where I sat against the wall, I could see Annie's pasture, the shed, and Annie, still polishing the old horse. From here, he looked just as dusty as he had before, but that could have been a trick of light.

Beyond the table were the work areas Mom had planned for her kitchen. I watched as she took hot rolls from the electric oven, slipped a crusty apple pie into it to warm while we ate. Her motions were quick and economical. She moved around the various work areas in precise patterns.

"I don't suppose you could tell me what made Annie pick that horse," she said, after a bit.

I shook my head. "Dad tried to talk her out of it. I think she felt sorry for it."

"That's logical—but not much reason for getting a thing like that in place of a riding horse. You haven't said much, this afternoon."

"No," I said.

Mom kept on working. When I didn't say anything else, she turned and looked at me. I shrugged. I didn't have anything nice to say. She smiled and turned back to the counter.

"Sam, Junior," she said. "I named you wrong."

T.C. came down the stairs and slid behind the table beside me. "Hey, Petey, how's things?"

"Great, T.C. You were so deep in the books I didn't want to bother you."

"That's true," he said. "I have put myself into that history, today. I know more about Sam Houston, now, than I ever wanted to know—but I bet that I'll pass that test on Monday."

"Will you get full credit for the course, if you pass this test?" Mom asked.

"Yes. It's a special thing arranged for me by Mrs. Thompson. She knew I would have to have a credit in Texas history to graduate, so she and Evan and several others have coached me this semester. If I can pass this—*when* I pass this," he corrected himself, "I will get full credit for the year's work. It is good of them, yes?"

"It is good of them, *yes*," Mom affirmed.

"Tell me about Annie's A.P.H., Petey," T.C. said. "Is he exactly what she wanted?"

I shook my head. "Not exactly."

From our bench, we could see her come from the shed, the old horse walking with her, his head draped over her shoulder. When she closed the gate behind her, he pressed against it, then hung his head over and nickered after her. He looked as if he expected to come into the house with her.

"Looks as if you made a fast conquest." Mom smiled at Annie as she came into the kitchen.

Annie looked at me uneasily. But when she saw everyone was easy and relaxed, she knew I had said nothing about our fuss. She smiled at me apologetically.

"Looks like it, Mom. I guess he's always had lots of things going on around him. He feels lonesome out here."

"He hasn't had time to get lonesome yet," Dad said, coming into the kitchen.

"When he fattens up some, he really will be beautiful. He has such pretty markings."

"But he's really awful-looking now," I said to her. She made a face at me . . . but not a mad face.

"I don't believe that Annie would choose an awful-looking horse," T.C. said in his softly accented voice. He was smiling at her across the table.

Annie got that hooded look on her face, even though she smiled back. "You have to come out after supper and see for yourself, Taro Chan."

"Yes. I want to. I have had enough of studying old things for a while."

I couldn't help laughing out loud. Annie got very red in the face, and T.C. looked from one to the other of us and finally at Dad, completely puzzled. Dad was suspiciously near to grinning, too.

"I don't know what I said that was funny," T.C. said.

"Well, the horse is rather old," Dad said. "Still, Annie's going to have to get used to that and not be sensitive about it."

"I'm beginning to realize that." She sounded sad. "Petey, lay off the sniggers, will you?"

T.C. kicked me hard under the table. "I did not intend any reference to your horse, Annie," he said.

"I was talking about the history. If I pass this test Monday, I have a credit made."

Outside, the old horse nickered again and rattled the gate.

"I'll tell you who has it made." Dad winked at Annie. "A retirement home and a personal hand-maiden to attend his every whim."

"Don't eat so fast, " Mom cautioned Annie. "He isn't going anywhere."

"Did Petey tell you that your evzone friend came to Annie's rescue this morning?"

"Evzone! Evzone! He's no warrior. Just an arrogant Greek chauvinist. He thinks every girl in school is chasing him," Annie said with unnecessary heat.

"He looked like a warrior to me this afternoon even if he had on jeans instead of one of those white pleated tutus. How could they fight in those things?" I asked Dad.

He shrugged. "Different times, Petey. I guess the puffy sleeves and pleated skirts all had a purpose at one time. Now, it's just a costume, like gyrene blues."

"Or Navy whites," Mom said.

"I've seen a lot of red stuff on some of those Navy whites. Makes it hard for me to think of them as a costume," Dad said.

T.C., who had been silent, said, "I think I am not following this conversation very well. I have been deep in my books all day. Was there a fight? Tell me. Evan came to your rescue? How?" His dark eyes flicked between Dad and Annie as they told him the events of that morning.

"He is a good person," T.C. said, when they finished. "I do not think I'd like to fight with him."

"Looked to me as if he'd have enjoyed tangling with those guys from the truck," I said. "Do you always pick tigers for friends?"

"It is the tigers who survive." T.C.'s voice was sober, even though he smiled.

"You looked like you wouldn't have minded, either," I reminded Dad.

Dad laughed silently, widely, in a way that made his ears flatten against his head.

Mom looked at him with her chilled-ice glance. "I didn't send you off this morning to get into a brawl."

"It wasn't a real brawl, Mom," Annie said soothingly. "Just a little misunderstanding about who bought the horse. Evan did delay them until Dad arrived."

"Well," Mom said, still unsatisfied, "I can't imagine fighting over that poor old thing."

Spots of color showed in Annie's cheeks. Dad shifted the talk slightly. "Annie, why don't you introduce T.C. to your horse before you do the dishes. Then he can help Petey with the little calves before it gets dark."

The supper dishes were always Annie's, but I usually helped with them. Today, I didn't think I'd offer to.

The old horse nickered when he saw Annie coming outside. When she opened the gate, he pushed his head against her, making funny little noises as if he were greeting her.

"It does not seem possible he would know you so soon," T.C. said.

The old horse turned to him and sniffed his chest, blowing through his nostrils in noisy whuffles.

"Why is he doing this?" T.C. said uneasily. He had no experience with horses.

"He's just getting acquainted," Annie said. "He does that with everyone he meets."

"He will know me the next time?" T.C. cautiously patted the Chief lightly on the wide part of his jaw.

"I expect he will. Here . . . do this." Annie showed him how to scratch under the throat and between the jaws. The old horse sighed and closed his eyes, leaning his head against T.C.'s chest.

"He does have nice markings, Annie. Though I was expecting a horse with white stockings," T.C. said, continuing to scratch.

"The A.P.H.? No, he isn't that, is he?" She laughed. "Funny, though, how he seemed to know me when I walked up to him. He came right over. I wanted him as soon as I saw him. He wasn't like anything I had pictured, but I wanted him, anyway." Unsmiling, she said, "Mom keeps wanting a reason that I picked him. I don't have anything I can pin down. Do people have to have reasons for everything they do?"

"I stopped looking for reasons, even for logic, a long time ago," T.C. answered. "Things will happen as they will, even though science always looks for reasons. Perhaps it is the spirits who direct our lives, as my people believe."

"You believe in spirits, T.C.? Like ghosts?" Annie frowned.

"Of course. For everything, there is a spirit that does not die. Is it not so in your religion?"

"Whoa. I don't want to get into a religious discussion, the way you and Daddy do. I do believe in people's souls. Tree spirits . . . rock spirits . . . animal spirits . . . I don't know about that. I read somewhere that spirits of the dead stay with us and guide us. It gives me a creepy feeling to think about it."

"Only if the spirits are bad do we need to be afraid," T.C. said.

"Yeah," I put in. "But how do you tell the good ones from the bad ones?"

"Ah." T.C. backed away from the horse and put a hand on my shoulder. "It is with the spirits as it is with the living. We take what we see and hope for the best. The spirits who directed Annie to her horse were good spirits, I think."

"Good for old Dogmeat, anyway," I said. "Come on, before it gets dark, we have to take feed down to the calves."

We turned to go, but Annie stopped us. "Thanks for the flowers, T.C. That was you, wasn't it?"

He smiled at her over his shoulder. "Perhaps it was the spirits."

9

The seven Angus calves were Dad's pride. They were also T.C.'s responsibility . . . and mine. We hadn't had them long. Two months or so, and already they had developed personalities as individual as those of people. The little bull was already feeling his responsibilities and his importance as the future father of our herd. He was the first one to taste whatever food was put out for his group. Also the first to greet anyone who come into his pasture. His name was MacTavish, Mac for short. The heifers were Anise, Licorice, Chocolate, Brownie, Coco, and Tar Baby.

They were kept away from the larger herd of Herefords in a small pasture we called the Gopher Field (for obvious reasons). It had raised a great crop of gophers every year since Mom could remember. Now we had greater ambitions for it. We'd spent a lot of time trapping the little rodents down to a reasonable population. We'd harrowed the field, smoothing out their mounded burrows, and now it was even and covered with grass. To get to the Gopher Field, we drove the tractor through the front pasture, across the shallow creek, and up a steep bank. I drove, T.C. standing behind on the drawbar and hanging on to the seat.

The calves weren't hard to find. Although there were thick woods to hide in, they knew the sound of the tractor . . . and that that sound meant feed pellets. There were six shadowy figures standing at the wire gap when we drove up. Mac was slightly apart from the girls. He knew where the food would be put down. T.C. had to shoo the heifers back when he opened the gap, so I could drive in.

We kicked hay off the little trailer in a short line, so each calf would have room to eat without interference from its neighbor. Alongside the hay, we dropped a line of hard pellets. In spite of our precautions, there were several head buttings over choice piles of hay before they finally settled down to eat. While they ate, we rubbed their backs and talked to them, to get them used to the sounds of our voices and to being handled. Someday, they might be show-class calves. Their blood was certainly good enough.

"You really like it here, don't you?" I asked T.C., after watching him run his fingers through the black curls of the little bull's back. He was crooning something in Vietnamese, I suppose it was, to the critter.

"Of course I do. Why would I not?"

I shrugged. "I don't know. Sometimes I try to think what it would be like to leave Dad and Mom and go to live somewhere where nobody spoke my language and everyone looked a bit different from me."

"Petey, it's funny. I forget I don't look just like everybody else. And English has been my main language since I was about ten. It comes naturally, now, though I still have trouble keeping up with the slang words."

"But don't you miss your parents?" I persisted. It was something that had worried me for a long time.

"I think about them, sometimes, what tiny bit I can remember. But that is so little! Your father is my father, now, and this is my home. You are my brother. I suppose I want to forget that other place. I have a lot of things to forget."

"Like your real name? Dad said you were too little even to know that, when you were found, but I'd think you might get a hint of it, sometimes."

"I remember a name. I'm not sure it was even mine. It could have been a name I heard somewhere later. Anyway, it wasn't important to me, anymore. Sister Toyoko had already started calling me Taro Chan, and after a while everyone called me that. It was as good a name as any."

"Isn't Chan a Chinese name, as in Charlie Chan?" I asked. "Why don't you take an American name?"

T.C. shrugged. "I don't know if it's Chinese, or care. It's American now, like T.C. T.C. Braeden is a pretty good American name. As you have reminded me, I do have an Oriental face. Better to have an Oriental name. Most Americans wouldn't know a Japanese name from a Chinese or any other Far Eastern one, anyway. Unless they served in Korea or 'Nam." He slapped the little bull on the rump so hard that it jumped and trotted away a few steps. It looked around at him reproachfully, before returning to eat more pellets. "I'm glad to be here, to have a mother and father. I like going to school, and I enjoy my friends there. You've been great. I only wish . . ." He didn't finish, and I knew what he was thinking.

"Annie?"

He nodded.

"I don't know what's wrong with her," I said. I think I must have sounded as disgusted as I felt. "I think it's that bunch she hangs out with at school. They're a gang of snobs."

"Tanya!" T.C. shook his head. "Evan likes Annie. She is friendly enough with me, but I have the feeling sometimes that she doesn't mean it. Like tonight. Annie showed me her horse very politely, but I had the feeling she would rather not."

"Dumb girls!" My teeth were clenched.

"Not just girls. There are some boys, too . . . but I do not expect everyone to be my friend. Nor do I really want that. It does not matter. But I do care whether Annie likes me. I wish it could be more than an armed truce with her."

"She'll come around," I said, wondering if she would. "Just ignore her."

"I've been trying that for a year. Still, there is not much else I can do, is there?" He shoved a couple of heifers out of his way. "Come. Let's walk the fence to check for loose wire and posts. I told Sam we would do that this week."

I followed him as he pulled on the posts, testing and checking for loose staples along the wire. We found where the calves had pushed a post until it wobbled in its hole and would need to be reset. On the creek side, where the fence was a part of the old original fencing, the wire was rusted and loose in two places. I used a piece of white rag from under the seat of the tractor to tie on, marking the spots that needed repairing.

A rustle at my feet made me jump. I saw the glistening hump of an armadillo, followed closely by four smaller shapes. They moved like clockwork toys, and you almost expected to hear a *click-click-click* as their tiny legs worked.

"Armadillo," T.C. said. He laughed. "Do you know what I read about them? They always have exactly four babies, no more, no less. And the four are always either boys or girls, never mixed. Very odd."

"Are they good to eat?"

"Bobcats love them. I read that people used to eat them, too. I'd have to be very hungry to try one, though."

The south end of the Gopher Field ran into the trees of our Deep Woods. About a hundred acres was part of the timber forest owned by a big timber company. It butted up against ours, and we were glad they used selective cutting and kept their woods wild. In the fall, they allowed hunters to come into their woods to hunt for squirrel and deer. Sometimes the deer came into the pasture with the Herefords or the Angus calves to browse. And sometimes they jumped into the hayfields. We didn't want them there. Dad always clapped his hands loudly and chased them out, knowing that they'd be back later. Still, he didn't hunt or allow hunters on our timberland. When he posted the land, he said, "I've had enough of killing. I would rather have live animals around."

Once, T.C. and I had seen a bobcat by the creek . . . only for a moment. As soon as he heard us, he turned and flashed his round golden eyes in our direction. Then he slipped, ghostlike, into the shadows and disappeared.

"Like the tiger." T.C. had laughed. "You can stand next to a tiger in the forest, and you won't know he is there until he opens his eyes and looks at you. Of course," he added, "sometimes you do not see his eyes until he has you by the leg."

"Did you ever see a real tiger? I mean loose? In the forest?"

"Twice. Fortunately, both times they were frightened by gunfire and were moving away when I saw them. They came after the battles sometimes and dragged bodies away, they tell me. It is easier than hunting in a forest where most of the game has been killed or driven off. There were many people in Thailand who, like me, had been forced out of Vietnam. They told tales that would curl your hair."

"That's terrible," I said.

T.C. shook his head. "No. I don't think so. We have ruined and destroyed so much of their hunting ground, all over Vietnam and Cambodia. There is, in everything, the wish to live. First it was the tiger's jungle. I do not think it is terrible . . . it does not matter to the dead man, and the tiger needs food, just as we do."

"That's a strange way to look at things."

"Different. Not necessarily wrong."

I had to agree with that, but I filed the conversation away to ask Dad about, when I had a chance.

I was thinking about bobcats and armadillos and tigers when T.C., who was driving the tractor back to the house, stopped. "Listen!" he said.

From the darkness of the woods at the lower end of our pasture came the sound of a pack of dogs on the hunt. Hounds belled through the woods, after some small creature. They were probably deer dogs. It wasn't illegal in our county to hunt with packs of dogs. Many people, like Mr. Blackburn, whom we had met that morning at the auction, raised and trained dogs to hunt, chasing the deer out of cover so the hunters could shoot them. It didn't seem very sporting to me, even though there was something exciting about hearing the dogs as they yelled, unseen, after their quarry.

I had my arms around T.C.'s waist, and I felt him shudder. "I do not care for hunters," he said. "Two legged or four legged."

We listened until the dog pack faded into the woods. Then we started up the tractor and went home.

10

Light spring rain fell through the night and into the next morning, just hard enough to make everyone want to turn over and go back to sleep. I heard Dad get up early. Then I heard the tractor. He had gone to feed the Herefords. Mom was teasing him about being an otter. All those years in the underwater demolition team had made him impervious to rain. And it was true. He didn't seem to mind getting wet at all.

Annie did. She hated to get wet, but in spite of that, I heard her slip from her room and out the door. Going to check on her horse, I guessed. She didn't try to ride him until much later in the day.

T.C. didn't come home after church. Instead, he stayed in town to have lunch with Evan. They planned to go over that history one more time before the big test tomorrow. I read until my eyes started to water, then I wandered out looking for Annie. She was tightening the blanket saddle around the Chief's back. The sun was coming out.

"I didn't think you were going to ride him," I said, rubbing his nose.

"I didn't think it would hurt to try him out, just to see what he can do. He might not be so bad," she said.

Annie mounted easily from the fence, sliding onto his back so lightly that he didn't seem to notice. As before, he seemed to straighten up once she was on his back, pointing his ears sharply forward and pulling in his lower lip so it didn't hang down. With his head up and his chin tucked back, he stepped out in an elegant parade walk, his knees springing high, his hooves snapping out smartly. There was a loud clicking sound when his weight shifted from ankle to ankle, but I didn't laugh. He was trying.

Annie rode out the gate and out of sight down the curving drive. From where I stood, I could see the Chief's sides start to heave before they disappeared.

The barn cat brought her kittens out into the afternoon sunshine, and I played with them for a while, waiting for Annie to come back. When she didn't, I began to worry.

A pickup turned into our road and stopped beside

me. "Hi, Petey. Where's your dad?" Dr. Kurt stepped out of the truck and stretched.

For a big man, he was graceful. He looked big enough to handle a full-grown steer, which he had done in his rodeo days in college. Yet now, when he picked up the calico kitten I'd been playing with, she didn't seem at all out of place in his big hands. I guess that's what made him a good vet.

"He's in the house. I'll go get him."

But there was no need. Dad had heard the pickup drive up and came onto the porch. "Hey! Have time for coffee?"

Dr. Kurt handed me the kitten and walked toward the house. "Sorry, not this time. I came to get the trailer. Have to pick up some calves to make some lab tests. Come with me, won't you?"

"I'd like to," Dad said. "Wait a minute." He went into the house while I helped Dr. Kurt unhitch the trailer from our pickup and attach it to his.

When Dad came out, he had on a clean shirt. His chin was smooth, and a trace of powder remained where he had quickly run the razor over his face. He smelled fresh and limey. It would be a long time before I could shave, but I liked to splash on some of that lime-scented shaving lotion once in a while, anyway. Maybe it might make the whiskers grow faster!

"Where's Annie?" Dad asked, looking at the open gate. He turned to Dr. Kurt before I could answer. "I'd like you to see the horse she picked. You won't believe it."

"Did she find that perfect horse?"

"Not exactly," Dad answered. "I want to see what you think."

"*I* think she's a nut," I said. "She went riding a long time ago. Ought to be back soon."

"Riding?" Dad looked at me with an odd expression and turned back to Dr. Kurt. "Well, you can look him over when you bring me back. Want to go along, Petey?"

I didn't. If T.C. didn't return soon, I would have to feed the calves by myself, but before I got around to that I wanted to see what was keeping Annie.

When the trailer bounced out of sight, I got my bike from the barn and pedaled after Annie, following her horse's hoof marks in the damp sand of the road. The track was easy to follow. When she had reached the hard-surfaced road outside our gate, she had turned toward the woodlands, riding along the wide shoulder of the road. The Chief needed to be reshod, and the hardtop would have hurt his feet. By the time the tracks reached our fence line, there were long scuff marks for each front hoofprint. Not quite a mile, and he was too tired to pick up his feet.

At the wooden bridge, which crossed the spring-fed creek in which we sometimes swam and fished for bream, the tracks led off the road. I knew I would find them at the clearing, where the creek ran shallow over clean white sand. There the pines made a kind of umbrella of shade over everything. The rain had cleaned the air, making all the scents of the woods stand out sharply. Rain, too, put the birds to drying their feathers busily. Many were hunting insects that were out drying their wings. Wet bushes slapped me as I turned off the road and into the clearing.

The Chief stood in the creek, in water up to his ankles. Annie knelt in the water and splashed it up on his legs, rubbing them. He reached down and snuffled the back of her neck. I could hear her talking to him.

"Hey!" I called. "What are you doing?"

Annie straightened, not as glad to see me as the Chief was. He nickered a greeting. "I'm giving him a rubdown," Annie said. "What does it look like?"

I shrugged, dropped my bike, and found a reasonably dry spot to sit upon on the creek bank. "How does he ride?"

"Very slowly." Annie shook her head. "He started to shake about the time I hit the road at the gate. I rode this far, but he's all done in. He's just never going to be a riding horse, Petey."

"What good is a horse you can't ride?"

"Pete," Annie said, very sharply. Then she stopped. Instead, she shook her head again and said, "If I knew that, I'd try to explain it to you. It's just one of those things. Like they say in the cowboy movies, a person does what he has to do."

That didn't make any more sense than buying the old horse in the first place. I changed the subject. "Dr. Kurt came by for the trailer. He wants to see your horse when he brings Dad back, after a while."

Annie frowned. I guess she knew what he'd say. We goofed around there a bit longer, but I knew

I had to get home to tend the calves. Annie came with me. When we reached the road, the old horse Annie was leading stopped as if he expected to be mounted.

"Come on. I need the exercise more than you do," Annie said, walking on for a few steps.

He looked puzzled and finally shook his head before stepping out and catching up with her. He put his head over her shoulder, and she rubbed his nose, talking softly to him as we walked home together, me pushing my bike. It didn't seem right to ride, when she had to walk.

T.C. wasn't home yet, so Annie helped me load the feed for the calves. Then she went inside to help Mom with dinner, while I took the feed to the Gopher Field. The calves weren't at the fence to meet me. Even when I drove the tractor into the pasture, they didn't run up as they usually did but huddled nervously at the edge of the trees. They didn't seem to know me, after all the times I'd fed them. I had to walk after them, driving them in circles, edging them close enough to the hay and pellets until the food was practically under their noses. It was terribly different. Always, they'd been eager, seeming glad not only to get the feed but to see T.C. and me.

I couldn't see anything wrong with them. Once they realized that I was me and I'd brought feed, they huddled close to me, each one wanting to be stroked and talked to. Even Mac pushed close for his rubbing. They stopped feeding to follow me to the gate as I drove the tractor out. They must have been playing awfully hard, I thought, for the ground was cut up all along the fence from the actions of their sharp little hooves.

Dr. Kurt and Dad were back when I got to the house. I joined them in the Chief's pasture. I was curious about what Dr. Kurt had to say about the old horse.

He was bent over, touching some little white spots on the Chief's front legs. He called them cannon bones and said they were "firing marks," which showed the horse had sometime or other bowed those tendons. It was a kind of injury that happened to racehorses most often, but also it could happen to horses whose work required them to start and stop fast. Like rodeo horses.

"He probably had some careless handling, away back there," Dr. Kurt said.

Before he gave his verdict, he folded the eyelids back, studying each eye carefully. He pinched the lower lip gently to study the stubs of teeth.

"Annie," he said at last, "I think he has been a good horse at one time. A very good horse. He's an Appaloosa, probably a real reservation Appaloosa. It still shows in his lines. But he's done a fair amount of work in the past, and now he's ready to go out to pasture. He'll never be a riding horse again. Not what you've wanted and talked about for so long."

Annie didn't look at anybody, just kept rubbing the Chief's shoulder and sort of leaning against it. "I know, Dr. Kurt. I guess I knew that yesterday."

"Then, why?"

She shrugged. "I liked him. He liked me. I couldn't let them take him for dogmeat. I just couldn't."

Dr. Kurt looked over the Chief's back at Dad. I knew they'd made some kind of arrangement.

"No, I don't like the idea of the dogmeat men myself. Tell you what, Annie. I have a nice big pasture on my farm with fourteen good horses on it. One more won't make a bit of difference. Why don't you let me take him over to my place? You can bring my little sorrel filly, Dancer, over here and ride her. I may be able to put a bit of meat on the Chief and get him in riding condition, before the summer is over."

Dancer! Wow! I wouldn't give you a nickel for most of the horses in the county, but I'd seen that filly. She was the prettiest thing I ever saw. She was a tall horse, slim, with one long white stocking and three white socks and a snip of white in the middle of her nose. She had a long, light-golden mane, which floated when she trotted across the field, which she always did when anyone drove past her pasture. Dancer for old Dogmeat . . . Annie would have to be crazy not to take a trade like that.

The Chief wasn't used to long silences from Annie. He seemed uneasy, too, because of Dr. Kurt's probing attention. He pushed at Annie with his nose and whuffed his breath softly against her shoulder. Annie rubbed him gently. Then she smiled at Dr. Kurt, the way she does when her mind is made up.

"Thanks, Dr. Kurt. I really would like to ride Dancer sometime. But I don't think the old Chief would like being left by himself with just a bunch of horses. He hasn't been around horses in years. He likes people. I think he feels good, being with me. I do wish you'd tell me what to feed him, though."

"Annie"—Dad's voice held a bit of hopelessness—"I think perhaps you might wait a little before you decide. Kurt's offer is a generous one. You've wanted a good horse for so long . . . a riding horse."

The set expression on her face didn't change. Her voice said, "I'll think about it," but her face didn't agree. I knew she had already decided. She was going to keep the Chief.

While everyone was talking, Mom came out of the house, the baby toddling along beside her, hanging on to her hand. When he was close enough, he turned loose and got down to business on his hands and knees, rushing over to Annie. She caught him and swung him to her shoulder. He leaned over and grabbed the Chief's mane with both hands. Annie had to pull hard to loosen his grip.

The Chief turned his neck and sniffed loudly at the baby. Brad squealed and started on one of his foreign-language conversations. The old horse nodded wisely, as if in answer to the baby's questions. Everyone laughed.

"You may not have a riding horse, but he's going to make a first-class baby-sitter," Dr. Kurt said.

"I do believe he's laughing, too," Mom said, patting the Chief's neck.

I was standing directly in front of the horse, and I thought he winked. Blinked, of course. Horses don't wink. He did look contented, though, like a cat looks when she's purring. Horses don't purr, either. They just switch their tails and look as if they have the world and a dozen apples.

You dumb old horse, I said silently. *You old dogmeat, you. You ought to look contented. Here you've bewitched Annie and wrapped her around your pin-fired cannon bones. Good food to eat, a pasture of your own, no work. An old con horse, you are.*

I glared at the horse, who didn't notice. Then I stomped back toward the house. I didn't understand Annie at all anymore. Worse than that, here were our perfectly sensible parents, who let her act like a dumb girl! I bet myself they would never let me pull a stunt like buying that useless horse.

Wait until I was ready to buy my motorcycle! Not that I would buy a crock, as Annie had done, but they'd never allow me to do anything that dumb!

11

The phone rang just as I stepped up on the porch. It was for Dr. Kurt. Mom and Dad had moved slowly toward the house, and they met him at his truck as he bounded back out of the house, rumpling my hair as he passed me. I'm going to shave my head. It won't be stylish, but it will stop people from messing with it.

"Sam, you heard any dogs around here?" Dr. Kurt asked.

Dad shook his head. "Not near. We hear dogs, sometimes, in the woods. Hunting. Haven't noticed anything special. Why?"

"That was Tom Laney, just down the road from you. Wants me to come right over. He had a couple of calves savaged by wolves or by dogs. I'd put my money on dogs. Aren't enough wolves . . . and besides, they seldom attack big, healthy stock. Dogs will, though, just for the fun of it."

"T.C. and I heard a pack of hounds in the woods last night," I said.

"When? Where were you?" Dr. Kurt looked worried.

"When we went out to feed the Angus calves. They weren't really close. We listened for a while, but they went out of hearing without coming near us."

"The Angus are still over in that west field?" Dr. Kurt looked at Dad, who nodded. "That's pretty far away. If there are wolves or a pack of wild dogs out there, you might better bring them up to a closer pasture, near the house."

Dad nodded again. "Good idea. I'll cut that small pasture east of the house in the morning and tighten up the fence. The boys can help me bring them up when they get home from school."

Dr. Kurt agreed. "The Herefords are big enough to take care of themselves, especially with the big range bull you have. I'd keep the Angus up close, until we know what happened to Laney's calves."

When he had gone, Dad questioned me about the dogs we had heard. Finally, he said, "I want you boys to be careful in the woods. If there is a pack of wolves around, they won't bother you a bit. You'll never see them. But dogs are different. They are used to people—not afraid of them at all. They're used to livestock, too. They'll attack people, if they're mean

94

enough and wild enough. If you hear them, get on the tractor and come right home."

"I didn't hear them tonight when I was down there."

"That's another thing, Petey. When T.C. is off with Evan, you wait for me to go with you. I don't want either of you boys going down there by yourselves for a while. Buddy up, O.K.?"

"Can we take the twenty-two when we go to feed the calves?"

T.C. was an expert shot, as Dad was. Neither of them had ever seemed willing to teach me. Maybe now was the time.

Dad didn't smile. "I don't think it's necessary, yet. I don't want you shooting up the place before we're sure the enemy is out there. Let's don't pop off any friendlies."

"Everybody in school knows how to shoot, except for me. They shoot at cans and stuff."

"Yeah," Dad said. "Stuff like insulators on tele- phone poles and road signs and songbirds. You'll learn soon enough about guns, Petey. Don't rush it."

T.C. came home after I had gone to sleep. I didn't see him at all until morning. After breakfast, the three of us walked down the curving road to the bus stop to wait for the yellow school bus. It was seldom that we had to wait more than five minutes for it. It would wait up to five minutes for us, if we weren't there when it stopped for us.

The bus was seldom more than half full when it came to our stop, so we always had a good seat going in. Coming home was different. In the afternoon, the driver allowed the first and second graders (six or seven of them) to get on first and to sit close to him, up front. Everyone else had to take their chances on a seat, so I usually stood most of the way. I really didn't mind. It was kind of fun to hang on to the polished rail and sway with the motion of the bus. Of course, I was forced to gripe about it, or everybody would think there was something wrong with me.

None of Annie's friends rode our bus. Most of them lived in town, and they really looked down, more than a little, on the "country kids" who had to ride a bus, instead of being brought in their parents' cars (or driving their own!). So Annie usually sat with Brenda Marshall, who was on the large side. Annie is almost the only person, except for the little kids, who is skinny enough to fit on a seat with her comfortably.

Brenda had a pretty face and nice hair—kind of goldy-red and wavy. She let it hang down in waves and pinned it back with a gold-colored clip or tied it with a ribbon. It always looked nice, and she did too, fat or not. Her dresses and shirts were always crisp and clean, and she smelled nice.

The Marshall farm was a dairy, and Brenda had a collie dog with some pups. She was more friendly than Annie's other school friends, and I guess that was why I liked her more. She asked Annie to come over to see her nearly every day . . . and told her to bring me, so I could play with the pups! I think she'd have given me one, if Dad would have let me keep it.

This morning, Brenda was full of questions about the horse Annie had bought. I suppose everyone in school had heard about the A.P.H. and that she was finally going to get it. Brenda didn't seem to know about the rumble at the fair, because her questions were all about how he looked and how he rode. She had never had a horse and didn't seem to want one. She was sensible, as well as friendly.

Annie spent a lot of time describing the Chief as he had probably looked years ago. She went into detail about what Mr. Walker had told us about his rodeo background. She even said some things that I didn't remember, which is not like Annie at all. If Brenda ever came over to the house to see that horse, she was going to wonder what had happened to him. I poked T.C. in the ribs, but he frowned at me and looked straight ahead. So I sat still and listened.

Annie's bunch were waiting at the bus stop when we arrived at school. They surrounded her quickly, leaving Brenda outside their circle, as they always did. It made me sort of mad. T.C. stood back with me, listening to their talk. His face wasn't happy.

Ross Blackburn wasn't even willing to wait for the preliminary hellos to be said. "How's old Dogmeat?" he asked.

"If you mean the Chief, he's fine." One thing about Annie . . . she could always play things really cool.

"Oh, I think Dogmeat's a much better name for

him. It's so original," Cathy simpered.

Evan, who had pulled into the parking lot in his red jeep, parked and walked over to T.C. and me. Now he pushed his way into the group beside Annie. "There's probably a better name for you, too, Cathy," he said coldly. "I don't think you'd like to be called by it."

Cathy sputtered, and the group laughed. "Well, you saw the old thing. You nearly had to fight to save him from the dogmeat men. What would you call him?"

I saw Annie put her hand on Evan's arm to keep him from saying anything more.

"I don't care what you call him, Cathy. Petey calls him Dogmeat. But he's my horse, and I'll call him whatever I want to. Maybe Dogmeat would be a good name. It will remind me of what would have happened if I hadn't come along."

"If you hadn't come along," Tanya said, "you'd have gone to the auction and bought a real horse. Now how are you going to ride with us?"

"I can, when I want to," Annie said. "Dr. Kurt said I could ride Dancer whenever I like."

"It's not the same as having your own horse, though," Tanya insisted.

Ross laughed. "Well, when you get tired of nursing old Dogmeat, my dad can always use him."

Annie looked at him blankly.

"We've got eight deer hounds. We can always use a little more dogmeat." Ross laughed again, with an edge to his voice.

Evan's face became quite red. Annie's was pale. T.C. began moving into the group, and I started away, looking for a teacher. The bell rang, thank goodness, and the group began to break up. The last I saw of Annie, Evan was walking on one side of her and T.C. on the other. She was walking a bit jerkily, and she seemed to be as angry as I ever remember seeing her.

When we met at the bus that afternoon, Annie looked tired and on the edge of tears.

"You O.K.?" I asked.

She looked at me a minute before answering. "Sure, Petey. Hard day."

"That bunch tease you all day?" I clenched my fists, knowing there wasn't a thing I could do about it if they had.

"They were pretty mean. Even Tanya. It would have been worse, I think, but every time I turned around either Evan or T.C. was there. It was a bit like learning a new word—every time you turn around there it is in a book or a magazine. I never paid much attention to Evan before today, but he was everywhere I went."

"Who was?" T.C. asked from behind her. Annie turned around quickly and stepped back.

"Whoops, careful! You'll step on something important—me!" Evan said.

"Are you following me around?"

"What do you think?" Evan asked, grinning.

"I think I'm glad," Annie said, holding out her hand. Her "Thanks!" included both of them.

The little kids were on the bus and seated. The driver opened the doors to the mob. I hung back. No use getting caught in the crush.

Annie started for the door, but Evan stopped her. "Why don't you all ride with me today? If you're not in a hurry to get home, that is. I have to stop for gas."

I stopped in my tracks. Evan had driven T.C. and me home a lot of times, and I loved to ride in the jeep. Annie never had.

"If you don't mind," T.C. said, "I must get on home. The bus will arrive before you, my friend. Come on, Petey. We have to help Sam with the little calves."

I started to get on the bus, but Annie stopped me. "It's out of your way, Evan."

"About five miles, and it's a lovely day for a ride," Evan answered.

"If you really don't mind, I don't want to ride the bus today. I've had just about enough of people. We'd like to ride with you."

Annie didn't look at me, but she gave me a little push toward the jeep. She wasn't smiling.

"Take your time," T.C. said from the doorway of the bus. "I will tell everyone where you are. It will be O.K." He gave me some kind of signal that didn't register then, and I saw him explaining to the driver that Annie and I would be driving home with Evan. The driver nodded. He knew that T.C. and I rode with Evan at times, and that it was all right with Dad.

Evan handed Annie into the jeep elegantly, while I hopped over the back and sat on one of the boxes behind the seats. He was proud of this jeep, and it showed. He had painted it himself, a bright red. His mother had helped him re-cover the seats and carpet the floor with scraps of colorful carpeting. Evan kept the jeep shining clean. On Saturdays, he used it to make deliveries for his father's grocery store.

"Sorry there's no top," he said, reaching across Annie to the tiny glove compartment. "Here's a scarf my mother keeps to use when she rides with me. If you want your hair to stay on, that is."

"Oh, good!" Annie said and smiled at him. It was an odd smile. Not quite real.

Evan shook his head. "Rough day, huh?"

Annie nodded, her lower lip quivering.

He kicked the engine over and raced it a couple of times. "Noisy," he said loudly, leaning toward her. "We'll have to talk later." Then he looked back at me. "Hang on, podner!" he said, his eyes twinkling. We started off with a roar and a jump.

It was smart of him not to talk to Annie just yet. She was about to bawl, but I didn't know exactly why. Unless somebody at school had said something else about old Dogmeat.

In spite of the wheel-squealing start at school, Evan drove very carefully through town, staying well within the speed limits and obeying the stop signs and traffic lights.

"I pay for my own mistakes," he had explained

to T.C. once, when taking us home.

"How many tickets have you paid?" I had asked him.

"Not a one, yet. And I don't intend to pay any, either. I work hard for my money. I'm not going to throw it away on something I can avoid." He stopped for the third stop sign in a four-block area and added, through clenched teeth, "Even if the laws are stupid."

Evan had let me drive the jeep from the hard-surfaced road up to the house. It wasn't a long way, but it was long enough to give me a feel of the jeep. It wasn't any harder to drive than the tractor, at least at a slow speed. But I doubted that he'd let me drive today, with Annie along.

Evan pulled the jeep into a service station and had the tank filled. The attendant was busy filling other cars, so he checked his own radiator and tires while I sat in the jeep with Annie. I tried to make conversation, but she gave such short answers that I gave up and sat back.

Annie wasn't in a good mood. I thought she was crying, once, but she didn't sniff or rub away tears. Evan didn't say anything to either of us, though he looked at Annie out of the corner of his eye several times. I thought from the set of his mouth that he was angry about something.

Without asking if we wanted them or not, he stopped at a drive-in for drinks. It was one of those places that serve root beers in big frosted mugs, which is my favorite way of drinking them. It is a self-service place. Naturally, I was elected to go and get the drinks.

Service took a while, because it's just about every-body's favorite after-school place. When I carried the mugs back to the jeep, Annie looked as if she were really going to cry. Evan looked madder than ever. He was talking in a low tone to her. She would just nod, without answering. Whatever he was saying didn't seem to be helping much.

"Petey, go tell Chaney that I'm taking you two home. We'd like to take the mugs with us. I'll return them when I get back to town."

I didn't know Chaney, the guy who ran the root beer place, except by sight. I figured that Evan did. When I told him, he looked out at Evan, who waved back.

"Sure, kid," Chaney said. He lifted his hand to wave O.K. at Evan.

Riding with the drinks in the open jeep made the frosting melt off them too fast, but it was better than no drinks at all. The five miles out to the farm seemed very short. Too short. When Evan slowed to turn into our drive, Annie touched him on the arm and pointed down the road toward the bridge. "Can you drive down there first?"

"Sure," he said. "I want a chance to finish our con-versation."

He turned off the road into the little grove by the creek, at Annie's direction. He stopped under the pines. "It's pretty down here," Evan said. He cut the motor, and the silence under the pines surrounded us.

"I like to come down here," Annie said, getting

out of the jeep and kneeling on the sandy bank of the creek. She splashed the cold water on her face, getting her hair wet on the ends.

Evan climbed out and leaned against the front of the jeep, watching Annie. I scrunched down in the back and wished I had made them let me out at our road. It was still not too far to walk home, if they fooled around too long. I had to help with the calves before dark.

"Evan," Annie asked, a questioning note in her voice, "you really seem to like Taro Chan. Why?"

He laughed, startled. "What a funny question. Why not?"

"No, I want an answer. Why do you do so many things for him? You take him home with you lots of times. Drive him here from school. You study with him and come out here to work with him, when you don't have to. Why?"

Evan squatted down on his heels beside Annie, not looking at her but into the clear water. He swatted at the little minnows that raced out of his reach and circled curiously, just out of range. No use trying to hit them. They were too fast. I knew.

After a while, he answered Annie. His voice was slow and careful. "It's a hard question to answer, why you like somebody."

"Is it because he's a foreigner?"

Evan stared at her in surprise. "Why, Annie, I never thought about that. Maybe it is. I'm a foreigner, too, you know."

"You?"

"Sure. My dad came over here just after the war—the Second World War. He built up the grocery business. Then he went back to Greece to pick a wife. Grandfather wouldn't let Mother come to America until I was born. Said he'd never get to see his grandson any other way. I'm a naturalized citizen, just like T.C. will be, when he gets his papers."

"But you're different. You were raised here."

I could hardly hear his reply, Evan's voice was so quiet. "Not different, Annie. Just luckier." He was still for a long time, tossing pebbles into the water, always just missing the minnow he tossed at. In the quiet, I could hear the pines talking softly in high whispers, hear a blue jay calling, "Thief! Thief!" in the woods. I could hear the baying of dogs, the ripple of water, the plop of the pebbles. Finally Evan looked at Annie. "You asked me a hard question. Now let me ask you one. Why don't you like T.C.?"

Two pink spots came out on Annie's cheeks. She glanced at the jeep to see if I was listening, which, of course, I was. "I do like him all right. I mean, I try to be nice to him."

Evan snorted. "That's not good enough. Being nice to somebody doesn't count for anything. You are 'nice' to store clerks and servants, not to your kinfolks."

"He isn't my kinfolks!"

"That's what I mean. He's your adopted brother, a part of your family. But you won't accept that or treat him like a brother."

"Because he's not my brother. Petey's the only

brother I have. I never wanted any other."

"What about the baby?"

"Oh, well . . . he's a brother, too, but he's so little. He doesn't count, yet. Anyway, everybody loves babies."

"Not everybody." Evan shook his head. "I have an uncle who leaves home, every time my aunt has a baby. Doesn't come back until it's about a year old."

"I don't believe that!" Annie was aghast.

"True, though . . . and they have five kids. He likes them O.K. after they get bigger. Just can't stand babies. Suppose your dad had brought home a tiny baby, Annie. Would you like it any better?"

She drew a pattern in the sand with her finger, thinking. "I try, Evan. Sometimes I don't think it's T.C. that I don't like, really. He represents everything about war that I hate. Every time I look at him, I think about all the terrible things that have happened in that part of the world—Vietnam and Cambodia, and Dad getting wounded."

"You sound like Tanya. She's got snobs for parents, so you can't expect too much from her. Your parents are real people, Annie. Your dad is one of the finest men I've ever known. He served over there for years, and you don't blame him for it. If you do, you've really got your thinking fouled up. And it wasn't his own land. It *was* T.C.'s."

"Oh, now you sound like Petey. Anyway, I thought you and Tanya were steadies."

Evan pointed his finger at me and shot me with

his thumb. "Petey's a smart guy. You'd better listen to him, instead of that bunch you've been calling friends. No, Tanya thinks I'm going steady with Tanya. I'm not steady with anybody and not going to be until I finish college. Then"— he leaned back, resting his weight on one elbow—"I think I'll go back to Greece and get me a good, obedient little Greek maiden for a bride."

Annie couldn't tell if he was kidding, but she made a face at him. "Now you ARE kidding."

"Dead serious." He laughed. "And we're off the subject. It wasn't fair for you to blame T.C. for the whole set of problems in the Far East. He wasn't in the mess by choice. None of those people are."

"Neither was Daddy. But the scars on his legs are just as ugly."

"I don't think they're all that ugly," I said. Annie could be as nutty as she wanted to about T.C., but it wasn't right for her to take off on Dad. "Besides, it's time we went home. I have to help with the calves."

Evan helped Annie up. "Might as well. We're not communicating."

Which was an odd thing to say. They had talked and talked. As long as they talked about T.C., I had stayed quiet, hoping Evan could stuff some sense into her. After all, he had come to her rescue Saturday and again this morning. But I guess there was no use hoping. A normal girl would have flipped over Evan and would have been furious with me for breaking up their talk. Annie, who is definitely not normal, gave me what could only have been a grateful smile.

Evan shrugged in an "Anyway, I tried" gesture. I wondered if T.C. had asked him to talk with Annie. Odd. T.C. mostly worked out his own problems.

12

The Chief wasn't at the gate, as I had thought he would be. Instead, he was standing under the pine. Though he raised his head, shaking it up and down at Annie and whinnying as we drove up, he made no move to come to the gate.

"That was a short love affair." Annie grinned wryly at Evan as we climbed out of the jeep.

I wondered why he was standing so still. When Annie and Evan walked up to him, I trailed along. Evan began to laugh as they approached. Annie laughed, too. I couldn't see why at first, as I was behind them, but when they stopped I moved up. I laughed, too.

Brad had propped himself between the Chief's front

legs and was taking a nap. His head was resting against one hoof, and his arms were wrapped around the other. When Annie reached down and picked him up in her arms, he muttered and snuggled his face against her neck. He didn't wake up.

The Chief sniffed at the baby with his big nostrils flared in and out. He stamped his feet, probably to restore the circulation.

"I wonder how long he's been standing like that," Evan said.

Annie shook her head. "I wonder where Mother is. She never lets Brad out of her sight, unless someone else is with him."

They started back to the house. The Chief, seeing Annie's shoulder was occupied, stepped up to me and rested his head over my shoulder, instead. I rubbed his soft nose. "You *are* smart, Dogmeat. You'll take up with anybody, for a pat on the nose."

Annie looked back at me, shooting arrows with her eyes. "Don't call him that. He may not be a fancy riding horse, but he's a mighty good baby-sitter."

"And that's not bad," Evan said.

Annie rubbed her cheek against the back of the baby's red hair. "No, I guess not. He really is a special horse. That's what I wanted. A special horse."

"Absolutely Perfect Horse," I reminded her.

"No such critter," Evan said. "Not in man or beast. But each one has something special in it, one way or another. Just takes someone with special sight to see it."

"Each one special," Annie said thoughtfully. "You do see people like that, don't you?"

He shrugged and smiled. "Sure. You must, too; why else would you fall for a horse you knew you couldn't ever ride?"

"Because she's not always too bright," I muttered. Evan grinned back at me, though Annie didn't turn around.

At the gate, I tried to push the horse back while I closed it. He wasn't having any of that. He put first one big hoof, then the other, through the opening, while I pushed back. He wasn't rough, just definite. He wanted to come along, too.

"Annie!" I bellowed. "I can't make your horse stay in his pen!"

She looked back and chuckled, which didn't help my feelings much.

"Oh, let him come. He won't hurt anything."

"If he steps on any of Mom's flowers, she'll squash us both."

"He might eat 'em, but he won't step on 'em," Annie said.

I hoped she knew what she was talking about as I stepped out of his way and let the gate swing open. As soon as I started for the house, the old Chief forgave me and hung his head over my shoulder again. He wasn't a horse to carry a grudge.

Sure enough, he was careful of the flowers, putting his big feet neatly on the path right behind me. At the steps, I slid out from under his jawbone and jumped up onto the porch. He looked at me reproach-fully, but he didn't try to follow. He knew he couldn't go into the house.

Evan laughed from the porch. "Makes you feel like a dirty dog, doesn't he? Coming inside and leaving him out like that."

"He's playing on your sympathy," Annie said, as she disappeared into the house. We could hear her calling, "Mom! Mom, where are you? Taro Chan?"

She came back onto the porch with a crease of worry between her eyes. "I can't imagine where everybody is."

"Don't worry," Evan said. "They're around some-where. The station wagon's in the garage. Tractor's in the shed."

"Pickup's gone," I observed.

"Thanks, chum," Evan said and frowned at me. He was worried and trying not to let Annie know it. I began to get scared.

The baby began to struggle to get down, and Annie made him a lap to sit on. He rubbed his eyes and stared at her sleepily. "Ann-eee!" he said, his voice as sleepy as his eyes. Then, "Horseee!" and that was excited.

"Horsey is right outside. And I do wish you could tell me what you were doing out there and where Mother is."

He made a hungry noise, and Annie said, "Petey, get his cup and pour some milk in it."

I had done that many times. Brad took the cup and crawled three legged to the screen door, patting on it to be let out. When no one opened it, he sat down and began to chatter to the Chief through the screen in his own peculiar language.

"He's mighty good-natured when he wakes up," Evan said. "My little brother is such a grouch."

"He's in a good mood today. Not always. I think he knows he wasn't supposed to be outside with the horse, and he's not pushing his luck." Annie took a can of lemonade from the freezer and then put it back. She didn't seem to know what her hands were doing.

"Mom just has to be around somewhere," I said. "She wouldn't go off and leave Brad alone for long."

"Go look in the barn, Petey," Annie said. "I'm going to phone some of Mom's friends to see if she has called any of them."

Evan latched the screen door behind me, so the baby couldn't get out. "Look, Petey!" he said.

Through the trees, I got a glimpse of T.C. flying up the road. "It's T.C.," I said. "Where's he going?"

Evan pushed past me and ran onto the porch. "T.C.! Hey, T.C.!"

If he heard, he gave no sign of it. A red pickup turned into the road, and the driver slowed enough for T.C. to leap aboard. Then it took off at full speed across the field toward the Gopher Field.

I looked at Annie. She was as pale as I felt. "That's Dr. Kurt's truck," I said.

"Let's go see what this is all about," Evan said, scooping the baby up and putting him in Annie's lap as soon as she was in the jeep.

113

I led the Chief back to his pasture, and they picked me up at the gate. The Chief didn't object, this time. He hung his head over the gate and watched as we drove down the road and through the gap. He nickered once, behind us, complaining that he didn't like being left behind.

Evan followed the pickup across the pasture, splashing through the shallow creek, spattering us when he slowed to shift gears for the steep climb on the the other side. It had never seemed steep, coming at it slowly on the tractor. For the fast-moving jeep, the clay bank was an obstacle, as it must have been for the pickup we were following. Deep ruts had been gouged into the bank as it had gone up and over.

As we cleared the top, we could see the red truck behind a thin line of pines in the Gopher Field. The wire gap was open.

Two of the heifers huddled in a corner of the field, eyes wide, hides quivering. They were snorting. We didn't see any people until we stopped by the pickup. Dad, Mom, T.C., and Dr. Kurt were bent around a stuggling black calf on the ground. Dad was down beside the little bull, his knee on its neck, trying to hold it still, while Mom stretched one hind leg to full length and T.C. held the other. Dr. Kurt knelt beside the calf, working over him.

Evan leaped from the jeep and reached around Mom to take the leg from her. "Let me," he said. She turned loose and stepped back, as he took the strain.

"Mom . . . what's happened? What's the matter?"

Annie's voice was high and shaky, and I could feel my own legs quivering under me. There was so much blood on the ground and on Mom's dress, it was frightening.

"Honey, it's pretty bad." Mom wiped perspiration from her forehead with the back of her hand, leaving a dark smear. Her legs were splashed with the same bloody marks. "Sam heard the dogs again. They sounded close, so he came to see. He found the whole pack of hounds chasing the calves round and round the fence line, slashing at them all the time. One of the heifers was already down, and before he could scare them off, they pulled another one down and slashed the little bull. We're going to lose him, son. If Dr. Kurt can't stop the bleeding, we're going to lose him."

As we watched, the struggles of the calf became weaker and weaker. After a time, he was still. Dr. Kurt sat back on his heels and said, in a low tone, "I'm sorry, Sam. There just wasn't anything I could do. I tried."

Dad rubbed the short black curls on top of Mac's head. Then he stood, slowly. "I know, Kurt. I know." He looked at his bloody hands and turned away without looking at anybody. He walked over to the creek to wash his hands. He stayed gone a long time.

T.C. and Evan gently loosed the legs they were holding and stepped back. T.C. put a hand on my shoulder. "Easy, Petey. You look sick."

"So do you," I answered.

"I'm sure that is true. I feel sick," he said.

"Did you see the dogs?" Dr. Kurt asked Mom.

"No, but Sam got a good look at them. He said he thought they were going to tackle him, too, but they finally turned and ran into the woods when he yelled and threw rocks at them. He came to the house for the first-aid stuff and called you, and we left the baby asleep in the house and came to see what we could do. We met T.C. as he got off the bus."

Mom was really shaken. Ordinarily, she didn't talk much. Now she couldn't stop. Dr. Kurt knew it, too. He patted her on the arm.

"Why don't you and Annie go back to the house? This is no place to have the baby." He didn't wait for her to answer, just walked her over to our truck. She stood beside it, uncertain whether to leave.

Dr. Kurt didn't argue. He expected to be obeyed. He walked over to his pickup and spoke into his CB radio. When Dad come up from the creek, he said, "Sheriff's on his way out."

"Not much point in calling him, Kurt," Dad said. "I saw the dogs, but a hound looks pretty much like any other hound. Nothing I can prove except for the fact of two thousand dollars worth of dead meat." His voice was husky, and his eyes were strangely bright.

Dr. Kurt shrugged. "He needs to know what's happening. You want to butcher out these calves? We could save the meat."

"No." Dad shook his head. "I couldn't eat it." He looked at Mom, and she nodded agreement.

"T.C., you and Evan go get the big tractor. Put

the ditching blade on it. We'll bury them over by that bunch of pines."

"Right," Evan said. "I need to call my folks and let them know what's happening. We'll take the ladies back to the house now, if you like."

Mom started to protest, but Dr. Kurt interrupted her. "I've already suggested that. Susan, there's nothing more you can do here."

"Kurt's right, honey." Dad came over and put his arms around Mom, holding her very tight for a minute, then leading her back to the pickup. "Go on to the house with the boys. This is no place for Annie and Brad. Make us some sandwiches. We'll be hungry after a while.

"Petey"—Dad turned to me—"go with your mother. When the sheriff's car comes, bring him here."

I had opened my mouth to protest at the first sentence. I shut it at the second and climbed silently into the back of the pickup with T.C. Mom, with the baby in her lap, and Annie sat up front as Evan drove the truck back to the house.

It was a silent ride.

13

The Chief whinnied as we drove into the yard.

"Your baby-sitter's calling you," I said to Mom. She looked questioningly toward Annie.

"You'll never guess where Brad was when we got home," Annie said.

"I left him asleep in the house when Sam called me," Mom said. "I knew you'd be along in a few minutes."

Annie looked sheepish. We had taken entirely too long in getting home, but she didn't mention that now. It wasn't a good time to tell Mom. "He was wrapped around the Chief's front legs. Sound asleep . . . or pretending to be."

"I was in such a flurry, I guess I didn't lock the

door. Didn't you find my note? I left one telling you where we were and why. I didn't want you to come down there and see that terrible thing."

"We didn't see any note," I said.

"I put it on the table," Mom said, looking to see if it was there and we had overlooked it, like a couple of dummies. But it wasn't.

We looked under the table and all around the kitchen. When I heard the tractor start up, I left Mom and Annie still puzzling over it. I ran out and jumped onto the back of the tractor beside Evan.

T.C. swung by the gate, and I dropped off and hunkered down to wait for the sheriff to show up. From where I sat, I could see Annie coming out of the house with a bucket and what looked like a handful of cookies. It reminded me of my stomach. It didn't seem right to feel hungry after what had happened to our calves, but I felt totally hollow on the inside. I couldn't even remember what I had had for lunch. The thought of a cookie made my mouth water and conjured up thoughts of hamburgers and fries.

Annie carried the bucket into the Chief's shed, and I guessed that it was full of warm water for the bran mash she fixed for him in the evening. I wondered how bran mash tasted.

The sheriff's black-and-white Olds drove through the gate, pulling to a stop beside me. The deputy slid over and made room for me in the front seat. "You Mr. Braeden's boy?" he asked.

"Yes, sir. Petey." I had never talked with a sheriff before. It gave me the same feeling I had had when

Dad had introduced me to his admiral. Dry mouthed, I didn't feel like telling him that he was driving too fast. When he came to the creek, he knew. I had never heard tires squeal on dirt before.

"Any other way to get there, Petey?" he asked, looking at the steep bank.

"No, sir. They're right over the rise on the other side of the creek, if you'd rather leave the car here and walk."

He looked at me as if he had never heard of walking and put the Olds at the bank. It was built low to the ground. It scraped bottom, whined, and teetered uncertainly on the edge. He gunned it just at the right moment, and it plunged over with a roar, almost crashing into a stand of pine seedlings before he stood on the brakes and stopped the car so hard that its back wheels almost came off the ground.

"That's good for the machine," he said. He glanced at me, grinned, and winked. "County buys the cars, boy. Every year. It's a good lesson for you . . . don't ever buy an old county car at an auction, no matter how good it looks. We drive 'em."

"Yes, sir," I said. "You sure do."

The deputy laughed out loud, and the sheriff's grin broadened. "Now where are those calves?"

I pointed him through the stand of trees, until he got a glimpse of the pickup. That was all he needed. They went over to Dad and Dr. Kurt, and I drifted over to where T.C. and Evan worked with the tractor, cutting deeply into the red dirt to make a place for the wasted calves. There was nothing for me to do

but watch. The two of them worked smoothly together, never getting in each other's way.

The four remaining heifers were huddled into a
corner of the field near the gap. They didn't offer
to move as I walked over to them. They snorted and
trembled as I came up. After I had patted them and
talked to them a bit, they gathered around me. They
lipped at my fingers and licked my bare arms, so I
knew that they were hungry. It was far past the time
when they were always fed, but nothing could be done
about that right now. Anyway, I knew Dad wouldn't
leave them alone in this pasture. He would take them
up to the barn lot for tonight, and they would go
more readily if they were hungry.

Except for the grinding of the tractor and the low
hum of voices by the truck, it was very quiet in the
woods. The night creatures, disturbed at the beginning of their evening's activities by our presence,
hadn't begun to make their twilight noises. The early
locusts weren't zinging away nearby, though deeper
in the woods their cousins were tuning up their eery
song.

The peeper frogs along the creek let nothing disturb
their singing, and after a while the bullfrogs added
their bass rumbles to the soprano peepers' air. A mockingbird, whose territory included most of this pasture
and the trees where the boys were digging, chacked
and fussed as long as he could stand it. But mocking-
birds don't hold grudges long, especially when they're
nesting. He finally left the low branches and flew to
the top of the tallest pine in his domain. There he

began singing to his mate, flinging himself into the sky for a barrel roll now and again, when some brilliant passage of his own song completely overcame him.

I watched his performance until the sheriff's car drove away, followed by Dr. Kurt's red pickup.

Dad came over and sat down beside me, watching the mocker too, for as long as we could see him against the sky.

"What did the sheriff say, Dad?"

He shrugged. "I described the dogs and he said about what I thought he would. Still, he does know a couple of men who let their dogs run loose most of the time. He's going to talk with them and look over the dogs. Kurt's going along. He might be able to detect something."

"It's not fair. People just let those dogs out to kill whatever they find. It's not fair."

Dad put his arm around my shoulder. "I don't think they turn the dogs out to become killers, on purpose. I guess they think letting them run loose will keep them in good condition for hunting. Dogs in gangs are like people . . . they get into trouble when they're bored and undirected."

He sighed. "Anyway, Petey, who ever told you that life was fair? It isn't fair, and if you expect it to be, you're in for a lot of disappointment. We do the best we can with what comes our way, and that's all we can do. Don't ever holler, 'No fair.' "

He looked over at me. "You remember that little statue I have on my bedside table? The fat guy riding the mule backward?"

I nodded. "The Chinese type?"

"That's the one. He's a Chinese god—very ancient. I forget his name, right now, but it isn't important. His followers believe that events, the things that happen to people, aren't important by themselves. It's the way people react to them that gives them significance. Do you understand?"

"I think so. It isn't what happened to the calves that's the important thing. Just what we do about it."

"Right!"

"What *are* we going to do about it?"

He grunted, and I could feel the muscles in his arms tense. In the darkness, it was hard to tell what his expression might be. I surely couldn't read his voice. "What would you do, Petey?"

That was hardly a fair question. I couldn't do a thing, and he knew it. I shrugged, remembered that he couldn't see me any better than I could see him, and said, "I don't know. Shoot every loose hound I see, I guess."

"I'm angry enough to do just that," he said. Then he sighed again and said in a voice I couldn't recognize, "But like it or not, we've moved to this country to live, and we have to get along with the natives. We can't shoot every gook who wears black pajamas . . . some of those gooks are friendlies."

I didn't know why that frightened me so much. Dad almost never spoke of his service in Vietnam, and then only to tell some story that was sort of funny. I couldn't remember the time when he had been over there—I was too small. But this talk of shooting gooks and the chilled ice of his voice shook me up.

"What are *you* going to do, Dad?"

"Nothing, Petey. Nothing. I guess that's what hurts most of all. I'm not a do-nothing sort of man, son. When somebody hits my people, I want to hit back. But this time I'm going to leave it to the sheriff. Let the law handle it. I'm going to do nothing."

I never thought of Dad as someone who could be pushed around. The bitterness in his tone was disturbing. "Three dumb old calves. I guess they're not very important."

"Three dumb old calves? They're MY three dumb old calves. The foundation of our Angus herd. You loved those dumb old calves, didn't you? I did."

I didn't say anything. He knew. Somehow, it didn't seem like enough, just leaving it to the law. I wanted Dad to do something. Anything. Anything except sit here, the suppressed rage making him shiver in the darkness, making me afraid. And my fear made me even more afraid, because I wasn't sure just which frightened me most . . . my dad's reaction or what had happened to the little Angus calves.

14

T.C. called from the darkness, "This is finished. Is there anything else to be done?"

Dad pushed himself up. "No, nothing else. Let's catch up the heifers and take them to the barn lot."

That took a little time. We tied halters of rope around their heads, and Dad and I each led two. They weren't used to being led, but they didn't fight or pull back on the ropes. They seemed to be glad to be going with us. To stay in that pasture by themselves, after what had happened, seemed to be the last of their ambitions. T.C. led the way on the tractor, lighting our way, and Evan followed slowly, patting a balky calf now and again when one hesitated. Then Evan went back and got his jeep.

We put down fresh hay and feed pellets in the lot, but the heifers seemed too frightened to eat. Instead, they huddled in the shadow of the barn, making soft sounds deep in their throats. They trembled when one of us got close, unexpectedly. I hated to leave them alone, but if they weren't hungry, I *was*.

Or had been. Until I sat down. Mom had made sandwiches, a big plate of them, and a pitcher of lemonade. There were peanut butter and cheese, my favorite; peanut butter and strawberry jam, T.C.'s preference; plain cheese with butter, tuna fish, and something on that round brown bread that I wouldn't eat if I were starving. The others, except Dad, were at the table when I came in. I slid onto the bench and took a peanut butter and cheese off the tray. Funny how the filling was heavy and sticky. Hard to chew and harder to swallow.

Dad came out of his bedroom, his hair dark and glistening from the shower. He had on clean jeans and T-shirt, but he was limping and looked tired to the bone. He took one of those brown bread things. He didn't eat most of it, just broke it up and pushed the bits around his plate while the rest of us talked.

"What did the sheriff say, Sam?" Mom asked him at last.

Dad shrugged. "About all he could say. Nothing useful. He knows about the dogs running loose, but proving which bunch of dogs is something else again. Almost have to catch them on the place."

"Dr. Kurt went with the sheriff to check some of

the packs. Maybe he'll find some kind of proof," I offered.

Dad looked at me, but he didn't answer.

"You've been watching too many detective shows on TV," Annie said. "Did you expect him to take pawprints?"

"They might have blood on them, or something like that," I said.

"Sam, you ought to put out poison for them," Evan said, very softly. "A pack gone wild like that is dangerous to a lot of things besides livestock."

"I've thought about it," Dad said, his voice cold and hard sounding . . . something like branches that are loaded with ice, when they break in the wind. "When I was a boy in South Dakota, the wolvers came through, putting out bait. They got about three wolves for every hundred coyotes, foxes, weasels, and other little carnivores they slaughtered. And then the rabbits almost ate us off the land. There was nothing left to eat *them*. Bait would be a good thing if only you could make certain you'd only kill the animal you're after."

"What is the bait?" T.C. asked.

"Usually strychnine," Evan answered. "Remember your chemistry? C twenty-one, H twenty-two, N two, O two."

"Ah, yes. Poison from the nightshade family. I do not think much of poison, either. But perhaps a pit in the Gopher Field . . . they will likely come back looking for the rest of their prey."

"You've just been digging in that ground, T.C."
Dad said. "You want to dig a pit deep enough to catch a dog pack in that stuff?"

"No. The ground is very hard. It is not a good suggestion."

"It's a good suggestion, but the lay of the land is wrong. For a pit to work, you almost have to be in a heavy jungle where everything travels in set paths. This is an open field. There's just no way to make sure the dogs would go near it."

"Why don't you just lie in wait and shoot the dogs when they come back?" Annie asked.

"Annie!" Mom said, reproachfully.

"No, that's a good observation," Dad said. "I'd like to shoot them, Annie. But I'm not going to do a thing, for a while. Give the sheriff a chance. We'll play it cool for a bit." He looked over at me. "But I'd say that a smart man would keep his dogs up, after this."

The phone rang, and Annie answered it. She called Evan, who went into the hall to take the call. "Evan's mother is worried about him," Annie said, as she sat down again.

"I don't wonder," Mom said. "It's been hours since he called to tell them he'd be late. It's after ten. Past bedtime, you kids."

Evan came in, grinning sheepishly. "Gotta go. Mom's breathing fire."

"I'm sorry, Evan. We shouldn't have kept you so long," Dad said.

"Don't worry. It's her Greek blood. By the time

I get home, she'll be crying. Probably she'll call over here to apologize for calling me. Papa says that with a Greek woman, you have to be a turtle with a thick shell—and know when to pull in your head."

Dad stood up and held out his hand to Evan, as he did with grown-ups. "Evan, thanks. The boys and I could have done it alone, but it was good to have your help."

Evan took the proffered hand. "I'm glad to help, sir. I'll bring everyone home right after school tomorrow. There may be something else I can do."

We all followed him out to the jeep. From the direction of the Chief's pasture came the sound of his shuffling footsteps. There was a soft nicker. Annie walked over to the fence and stroked his nose.

In the reflected light from the porch, Evan's teeth gleamed white. "See you," he said, and started the engine.

15

Out of the darkness, the monkey-faced owl who lived in the rafters of the barn in daytime and hunted at night flew up with a startled whoop. He sailed through the lights toward the safety of the barn. As he lighted on the long pole above the hayloft door, he gave his scary call that sent shivers up my spine. To the owl, it was his own way of reassuring himself that everything was all right and nobody was chasing him. But it made my skin goose pimple.

To the little heifers below in the barn lot, it must have sounded like the dogs. They let out a panicky bawl and all four of them hit the fence as one, splintering the wooden rails and scattering in different directions in the darkness.

One of them thundered past me, eyes red and rolling in the jeep's headlights. I grabbed for her halter as she brushed past, missed it, and caught her tail as her hindquarters hit me in the chest. Her momentum pulled me against the jeep, and I lost my grip. She ran on down the road, and I sank down, speechless with pain, beside the jeep.

Dad leaped after one of the calves, and T.C. ran after another, while Evan jumped from the jeep, trying to catch the one I'd missed.

Mom ran to me. "Petey, are you all right? Here, let me see."

When she touched my shoulder, I hollered. I couldn't help it.

Very gently, she put her arm around my waist and helped me to the porch. She was leading me into the kitchen when Evan came back through the lights. He had his calf by the halter and the tail and was forcing her ahead of him toward the barn. He had a skinned elbow, and the knees of his jeans were torn.

T.C. soon came with another, holding it the same way, halter and tail. He wasn't as battered as Evan. The two of them went looking for the fourth calf, and for Dad, after locking their two in the barn. It was some time before the three of them came back with the two remaining calves. They stopped by the porch.

"How's Petey?" Dad asked.

"I think his shoulder may be broken," Mom said. "It's a bad bruise, and the joint moves oddly. It's very painful, too."

"Yeah," I said. "It does hurt."

The heifers were slavering white foam from their mouths and moaning with fear.

"Poor little critters," Evan said. "I never thought I'd see a cow with hysterics."

"Honey, what are you going to do with them?" Mom asked. "You can't leave them in that dark barn all night. They'll go mad with terror."

"Put them in with the Chief," Annie said. "He likes little things. I think he'd be good for them."

Dad nodded. "I think you're right."

They led the frightened calves over to the fence, where the Chief was pawing and snorting. Immediately, he put his head over the fence rail to smell them. They mooed and struggled. Then they began to pull toward him, trying to touch him with their noses. Annie opened the gate, and the men led the heifers inside.

The Chief seemed excited to see them, nickering softly, touching their backs with his nose, moving around them. T.C. and Evan brought the other two from the barn, and the old horse included them in his examination. He began to bunch them, moving around them in a circle.

"They'll be all right with your baby-sitter," Dad said to Annie. "Let's leave them now."

As soon as everyone was outside, and the gate closed, the Chief took over, keeping them in a secure knot. He began urging them up the hill, pushing on their rumps with his nose, crowding them with his chest toward the shed. He snaked his head and shifted his feet, the way a cutting horse is supposed to, pushing them in the direction he wanted them to go, without rushing them. They disappeared into the darkness of the shed. In a little while, the troubled murmuring of the heifers stopped, and everything was quiet.

"I'll be damned," Dad said, not apologizing for his language.

"Now that the crisis is over, I have to go, or I'll have to be rescued myself when I get home," Evan said. "I'll see you tomorrow. Hope that arm's not too bad, Petey."

"It'll be O.K.," I said. But I wasn't really convinced. By then, the thing hurt so bad that I was beginning to feel light-headed.

Evan waved good-bye and drove off, his headlights swallowed up into the night before the sound of his engine died away.

Dad must have heard something in my voice. He came over and squatted down beside me. "Where do you hurt?" he asked.

"All over," I answered truthfully. "But I think my shoulder's busted."

"If you're trying to get out of school tomorrow, forget it," he said and laughed. His hands were very gentle as they explored the injured shoulder. He put an arm around me when I began to sag.

My knees felt like wet newspaper, and my stomach was kind of squishy. I wasn't going to cry, no matter what, but the tears began to squeeze out, in spite of anything I could do to stop them. I really did *hurt*.

"I don't think it's broken," Dad said. "But we're

133

going to the hospital to have some X rays, anyway."

I wanted to say, "Wait until morning," for everyone looked so tired. The words just wouldn't come out. I knew Dad wouldn't wait, anyway. And there wasn't much point in waiting, not if it was going to hurt like this all night.

Mom called the doctor while Dad went for the pickup. "Are you worried about staying here with the baby?" she asked Annie when she hung up the phone.

"No. Of course not. T.C. is here," Annie said. "We'll be fine."

"I'll sleep on the couch until you get back," T.C. said. "I want to be downstairs."

"That's a good idea. Annie, you might like to sleep in our bed, to be near Brad. I don't know if you could hear him from upstairs, if he wakes up."

"Sure, Mom. Don't worry about anything. Take care of Petey. We'll be all right," Annie reassured her.

The two of them helped me into the pickup, and I sat between them, Mom cradling the injured arm gently next to her, protecting it.

It was a drive without conversation. The only thing I remember anyone saying was when we were about halfway there. Dad looked at Mom and said, "Quite a day! Quite a day!"

"I can do without another like it," Mom agreed.

At the hospital, they were waiting for us. Dr. Jerry Tucker was a young guy, tall and lanky. He seldom smiled. His mournful expression was generally enough to frighten his patients into doing anything he suggested. I knew that I never felt like arguing with him.

He made me feel as if I were at death's door. He examined me in the emergency room, lifting my arm and probing the muscle of my shoulder and back with his strong fingers.

"Sorry to get you out so late, Jerry," Dad said, after the preliminaries were over.

Dr. Tucker sighed. "Nothing ever happens to any of my patients in the daytime, during office hours." I sucked in my breath sharply, when he came to the touchy spot. He left off probing immediately and stuck a needle full of stuff into my arm, before I had time to dread it.

"Can't stand jumpy patients," he said. He went back to examining the shoulder, probing and moving it, after he'd given the drug time to work.

When they finally took the X rays, I hardly noticed, and by the time they decided what was wrong with me I was too sleepy to care. I hardly remember being carried back to the pickup with about fifty yards of tape wrapped around my shoulder. One arm was pinned to my body, I do recall. I surely don't remember being put to bed. Not until he climbed down from the top bunk the next morning did I know that T.C. had switched beds with me.

"What time is it?" I asked, when I could shake the fuzz out of my brain.

"Time for me to get ready for school and you to go back to sleep," he said.

135

"I'm hungry." I struggled to push myself into a sitting position without knocking my brains out on the bunk above. "I don't know why you like this bunk better than the top one. It's too squeezed in."

"I don't like or dislike either one. It's all the same to me, as long as I have a dry place to sleep. I hate sleeping on wet ground."

"Well, I'm glad you haven't any druthers," I said. "I don't like this one. Did you do that a lot?"

"What?"

"Sleep on the wet ground."

"Petey, even once is too much."

"But you did it more than once, didn't you?"

"Yes, Petey. More than once. Does your shoulder hurt much?"

"Only when I breathe," I muttered.

"You must be feeling better. You're grouchy," Mom said from the doorway. "Step it up, T.C. Breakfast is ready. You'll miss the bus."

"What about me?" I asked.

"You're going to get a few days off." She sat on the side of the bunk and examined the bandages, to see if they were still tight enough. "Dr. Tucker calls it a separation, and he said that that is sometimes a lot more painful than a nice clean fracture. Not to mention that it's a lot more trouble to heal well. So, Pete-my-Buck, you may just finish this term of school at home."

"Can you really *do* that?" A little pain, I figured, was a small price to pay for my freedom.

"We'll see," Mom said. "Annie's going to stay

home with the wounded and lame today, while I go into town to see your teacher to see what she has to say about it."

I leaned back on the head rail of the bunk. If Mom was going to ask Mrs. Reilly, I'd just as well put on my pants and go to school today. She wasn't going to look favorably on any plan that would keep any kid out of school, even if every bone in his body was separated. Oh, well. One day off is better than none.

"I'm hungry, too," I reminded Mom.

"Not much of a nurse, am I?" She smiled, pushed the hair out of my eyes, and cleared a place on my forehead for a kiss. "Feel like coming to the kitchen, or do you want breakfast in bed?"

I scrooched back a little more. "Can I have scrambled eggs?"

"Whatever you want—if we have it."

"Biscuits?"

Mom nodded.

"And bacon?"

Her eyes were twinkling, as she nodded again. Usually, we had oatmeal or something like that for breakfast on school days.

"Can I have some honey and some . . ."

"Hold it!"

Mom was laughing, now. "Don't push your luck, Petey. I'll send someone up here to start you off with some orange juice. After bacon and eggs and biscuits and honey, you'll just have to take potluck with the rest of us, if you're still hungry."

"O.K.," I said and grinned back at her. "A guy heals faster, though, when he has lots of good stuff to eat."

She left, laughing. I heard her say to Dad as she walked into the kitchen, "I don't know where he gets it. Certainly not from my side of the family. Your son is getting to be a first-rate con man."

Dad said something I couldn't quite hear. They laughed together, in that comfortable way that makes a kid feel warm and safe inside. Even if they are laughing at him.

16

Annie brought up the orange juice.

"How's old Dogmeat today?" I asked.

"Don't call him that. He's suffering from a bad case of divided loyalties. I took him his bran, and he just took little nips out of the bucket, instead of sinking his head into it up to the eyes, the way he did last night. He's got responsibilities."

"The little heifers are O.K.?"

"Fine. They mooed at me and kept the Chief between me and them. Even when I was brushing him down, they stayed on the opposite side and peeped at me from under his barrel. You'll have to come down and see after a while. It is so funny!"

"Is Dad going to leave them in there with him?"

Annie shrugged. "I guess so. Why not? They seem to like it . . . they're pretty well settled down, as long as nobody is in there with them. I know *he* likes it. I put oats in his bin, and the heifers started eating it. The Chief just lipped at their withers, the way he does with my fingers. It didn't bother him a bit when they started in on his breakfast."

Dad brought in the white bed-tray, loaded down with food. "Hey, Petey! How goes it today?"

"Sore. Hungry. That looks good."

"Your mother can spread a pretty nice breakfast, when she gets going." He laughed and left me to eat one-handed.

There were more biscuits than I could possibly have eaten by myself. Not out of a can, either. She had warmed the honey. There was a pile of golden scrambled eggs that must have been four or five, at the least. Besides the four slices of bacon, there was a glass of milk. On the side were butter, peanut butter, and half a dozen of those brown sugar cookies I like so much. My appetite didn't need any encouragement. I was hungry enough to manage one-handed very nicely—without help!

Once things quieted down, I slept until noon. Then I struggled into my pants by myself, but I couldn't figure out how to get into a shirt. Mom helped me into an old sports shirt of Dad's. She put it on the good arm and then buttoned it around the taped one. I looked into the mirror. If I'd had an eye patch, I'd have made a pretty good pirate.

"Dr. Kurt drove up a little while ago. He and Sam

are down at the barn," Mom said. "Annie's out with the Chief. If you'd like to go outside for a bit before lunch, you may."

Stiff as I was, I still thought going outside sounded good. Eveything is so green and fresh in May. New leaves everywhere, new grass. Flowers growing wild in the woods and the pastures and the yard. There was even a trumpet-shaped flower, all red-and-gold-colored, hanging out of the trees. I stood on the porch until I located Dad and Dr. Kurt by the sound of their voices, inside the barn.

I stopped just outside, not because I wanted to listen, but because it was one of those conversations you ought not to interrupt.

"I don't want this to come to a killing," Dad said.

"Neither does the sheriff, Sam. Nobody does," Dr. Kurt said. "I just thought I ought to tell you. Blackburn seems a good enough sort, but he's a mean man. He has already killed one man over those damned dogs. He served several years in the penitentiary for it, too. People walk shy of him, now he's out. Treat him with a lot of caution."

Dad's laugh was a short bark that I didn't like the sound of. "Kill one man! Kurt, what do you think I did in the Navy for those twenty years? Sat safely at sea pushing a pencil? I cruised up and down those muddy, fever-ridden rivers with the patrols. Every few days—sometimes every few hours—Cong or Khmer-Rouge or Communist Thai would come bursting out of the jungle at us. I couldn't possibly count the dead men I pin on my chest every time I put on those five rows of ribbons. Even in the peacetime Navy there are hot spots, and as liaison with the patrols I was in the middle of them. 'Nam was the worst, but it wasn't the only.

"I wish I did have just one man to my account. Or none! That's why I want the sheriff to handle this thing. I don't want it to get too personal. I haven't been out of the Navy that long."

Dr. Kurt's jacket brushed against something as he shifted position. "Sam, I didn't mean that you couldn't do anything about it. I just thought you needed to know what kind of man we're dealing with."

"You sure it was his dogs?"

"Pretty near certain. There was a brindle bluetick, three Walkers, and a couple of redbones. Just the assortment you described. There were others, too."

"I didn't see all of them." Dad sighed. "I'm still going to let the law handle it, even if I have to go to court to make him keep the dogs up. I'm not going to let them chew up any more of my livestock, Kurt. I know ways to kill those dogs—tonight—so that nobody would ever know what happened to them. I don't want to do it that way. Not here. Not even with dogs. That's not what we came here for.

"Blackburn definitely said that he wouldn't pen them up?"

"Said he couldn't. Didn't have enough pens, and it ain't good for a hound to keep him tied all the time."

"Mine's not the only stock they've attacked. What's the fellow's name we stopped by to see the other night? Laney? I'll talk with him. See if we can get some kind of legal action going."

"And in the meantime, if they come back?"

Dad laughed again. That same ugly laugh. "They'll have to take their chances."

"You can't watch the stock all the time."

"I don't have to watch the Herefords. That old dirt kicker may look like a cube of fat, but he can handle anything that threatens his herd. Besides, they're fully grown. Those dogs haven't bothered anything but calves and young stuff. I'm turning the young Herefords out with the older stock for a week or so. I doubt that the dogs would come this close to the house to get at the little Angus heifers again."

"Doesn't seem likely," Dr. Kurt agreed. "What if they do, though?"

"The thirty aught six is in the kitchen, loaded. T.C. knows just where it is, and he's as good with it as I am. Maybe better. I expect Susan wouldn't be shy about using it, either, if she needed to. I think I'll call my lawyer this morning. See if I can go in this afternoon and talk to him about what steps we need to take."

Dr. Kurt laughed. "This is a very small community, Sam. I doubt that you'll have any trouble getting an appointment whenever you want it."

"Thanks, Kurt. I really appreciate everything you've done for us."

They were coming out of the barn now, and I didn't want to be found eavesdropping. I wandered across the back lot behind the barn. There was a little creek that, according to the man who sold us hay, had never been known to go dry. Once it had seeped all over the barnyard from a shallow channel, making a sort of marsh. Then it had spilled across where the front yard was now, near the house, and wandered away into the woods, through the pasture Annie had for her horse.

T.C. had taken that as his first project as soon as we had moved to the farm. All by himself, he had dug the channel deeper in the direction Dad wanted it to go. Then, together, the two of them had cemented those parts that seemed likely to wash and put gravel into the bottom of its muddy channel. Dad had had a pond dug in the big pasture, where we kept the Herefords. The creek filled that pond and kept it fresh, then ran away to wander freely through the woods beyond our farm.

At first, the pond had been red with mud. After a few months, it had cleared a bit, and now it was a good place to swim on warm afternoons in summer. The Herefords didn't seem to mind, either. Sometimes they joined the swimmers by wading deep into the water and making pointed remarks about creatures crazy enough to splash around in their drinking water. Only the bull sometimes objected.

Like today.

When I entered the pasture, intending to go down to the pond and sit for a while, he lifted his head and came over to see what I wanted. He wasn't ugly about it, but it was clear that I wasn't welcome. I left without any argument.

It didn't irritate me to be turned out of the pasture. It was the bull's business as a range bull to take care of his herd. "That old dirt-kicker," Dad had called him. Dad would stand beside him, rubbing the itchy places behind his horns and talking, while the bull rumbled softly in his throat, as if he were answering. It always looked as if they were discussing the herd.

Mom didn't like for Dad to make so free with the bull. She was afraid of him and said so frequently, though he had never in any way offered to hurt anybody. But she was right about one thing. It was wise to take care around him. He was just so darn *big* . . . he could step on you absentmindedly and squash you flat, before he even knew you were there. T.C. regarded him with admiration from a great distance. Annie never went into the pasture to swim unless Dad was along.

Mom called us for lunch. "Where *were* you?"

"Oh, just around," I said. No need to get her started. My going into that pasture without Dad was one of her pet peeves.

After lunch, Dad went to town, and Annie sat feeding the baby. I helped stack the dishes with one hand and tried to look pitiful. Mom ignored that. She always knew when sympathy was merited.

When we had finished, she asked, "Annie, would you mind staying close to the house this afternoon? I'm going to town, and I don't want Brad wandering around unsupervised. Your horse wouldn't hurt him, but the calves might step on him."

Annie laughed at the thought. "Sure, Mom. I have

to study, anyway. Can I take him out to the pasture with me when he wakes up?"

"If you're careful. The Chief has the heifers to look after, now. He might not have time to be such a good baby-sitter today."

"I'll be careful."

"I'll see that she is," I added.

"You. Go and lie down for a while." Mom pointed her finger at me. "You can get up when the baby finishes his nap."

Objections did no good. When I got all stretched out, I was glad Mom hadn't listened. My shoulder ached deep down, as well as twinging sharply when I moved quickly. It was good to lie back and relax.

There are noises on a farm to listen to when you are quiet on a lazy afternoon. If you don't want to lose yourself in a book, and there's no good music on the radio, and there's nobody to talk to, you can just listen.

Annie was in the porch swing. The chains creaked as she gently pushed herself back and forth. I knew she was deep in her studying, not even aware that she was moving. Cow sounds came faintly from the pastures, mingled with the voices of birds and the distant whine of trucks passing on the highway. There was just enough wind to set the trees to talking. The oaks and gums gossiped and chattered. The dignified pines shushed everything and sighed, occasionally, with what seemed outraged dignity.

I like the pines best. They stand so tall and straight and they mind their own business. That old pine out in the Chief's pasture is so large I can't reach around it. Yet it's a friendly-feeling tree, pleasant to lean against, with soft needles fallen around its base, for sitting on. It smells clean and resiny on a hot afternoon.

Some of the kids claim they chew the yellow, sticky gum that seeps out of sweetgum trees when you make a deep cut in the bark. I tried that once. It stuck to my teeth and didn't taste all that good, either. I'll take bubble gum or Doublemint, any day.

Beneath all the sounds I listened to, I was vaguely aware of another sound. It was too faint to identify, but it nagged at me like a name I couldn't remember, or the date John Adams became President. (I missed that on a test just last week.) The sound drifted around under all the other sounds, and finally it faded away. I forgot about it as I listened to the vocal battle between a meadowlark that had come too near the house and the mockingbird whose territory he had invaded. I finally drowsed off to sleep, listening to those nutty birds screaming at each other.

17

"Hey!" Annie was bent over me, poking my chest while one braid tickled the end of my nose. "Wake up! Brad and I are going out to the Chief's pasture for a while. Want to come along?"

"Sure. Anything to get out of the house. You through studying?"

"No, but the baby's awake. And the sun is gorgeous. A shame to waste a day like this studying. I can do the rest tonight."

"You going to school tomorrow?" I tested the stiffness of my shoulder and didn't think I'd be going anywhere tomorrow.

"I guess so. Unless Mom needs me at home."

"Your grades aren't all that great. Isn't it going

to mess you up, missing so much?"

Annie gave a funny little shrug. "I'm passing everything. I doubt that these few days will cause me much trouble. Next week, now, when we're reviewing for finals . . ." She didn't finish. No need to. That is one thing good about being in the lower grades. No finals.

Annie went out with Brad and left me to get up at my own speed. Which was a good thing, because my speed wasn't anything to brag on. I seemed to be getting stiffer and sorer, instead of better. When I finally got to the kitchen, I found the plate of cookies and the glass of orange juice Annie had left on the table for me. When I finished the juice and rinsed out the glass, I stuffed cookies into the pocket of Dad's shirt and followed her out to the pasture.

The baby was hanging on to one of Dogmeat's legs. The horse was lipping at the top of his head. When I came close enough, he reached out and blew on me through his big nostrils. I rubbed him between the eyes briefly, before sliding down beside Annie. I set my back to the big pine.

"It's nice out here," I said.

"Um-hum," Annie agreed, her eyes on her book. I shut up and watched Brad. It didn't seem like such a good idea, letting him wander around under the horse like that. But if Annie wasn't worried, I wasn't going to be. He wove in and around the horse's feet and front legs, babbling to him as if he expected to be understood. The four black heifers weren't willing to go far from their watch-horse. Still, they didn't want the baby close to them. They stayed just out of his reach, kinking their tails and making short runs away, when he reached for them. The baby crowed and laughed at their antics. He tried to coax them to play with him, but they weren't having any. It was a game to him. When he tired of it, he left the horse and crawled down the hillside toward the shallow creek.

"Brad's wading," I said, when Annie didn't seem to notice.

She grinned at me over the book. "I know. I'm watching. Won't hurt anything. Don't get your bandage wet."

It's hard to wade without getting wet. I walked down to where Brad squatted. He was getting his tail wet while he patted at the surface of the water, soaking himself. I made him some leaf boats and tried to communicate. He might have been a Martian, for all the sense he made. Still, for all his language problem, he was a pretty smart kid. He didn't smash the leaf boats. He followed them along, freeing them when they caught on the bank of the creek.

When one would finally race out of his reach or the breeze would capsize it, he would come back to me. He'd say something that I generously took to be "'Nother boap!" I would give him another "boap," and he would follow it until it, too, was gone.

We played by the creek for a long time before Annie came down. "You two come back up the hill and sit in the sun. I'll go make us some peanut-butter sandwiches."

"Put cheese on mine," I said.

"I know, I know. Come on, Brad. Out of the water."

"NO!" That was clear enough. He turned back to his last boat.

"Peanut-butter-and-jelly sandwich?" Annie said, with a promise in her voice.

"No," he said again, but not as definitely, this time.

"Peanut-butter-and-jelly and milk?"

"No."

"Peanut-butter-and-jelly and Coke?"

"O.K.," he said cheerfully. He waded out and followed me up the hill to the spot where the pine shade began. We sat in the sun, making a house out of the thick pine needles. We'd push them around to form rooms. The cones made fine furniture. It was mostly my project, with Brad handling the cones very gingerly. He didn't like the stickery points.

Old Dogmeat and the heifers came over to watch. They nosed at the needle walls and made doors where no doors were supposed to be. The horse finally came around to stand behind me. He breathed on my neck, with his nose resting on my good shoulder. It didn't mean anything, but it was kind of nice, just the same.

Annie came onto the porch with a big tray. Just as she started down the steps, the phone rang. She put the tray down on the swing and went into the house. When she came out, she was smiling.

At the gate she called to me, "Mom has a flat. She's going to be late getting home, and she wants me to start supper. Why don't you bring Brad in and put some clean clothes on him, while I get started?"

"One handed? I can't dress him when I have both hands free and a knee in his chest. Where's my sandwich?"

"Well, peel him down and dry him off. I'll do the rest. Come in to eat your snack. I ought to make something for the boys. Mom said she saw Evan and T.C. pass the station. They'll be home in just a little while."

I coaxed and dragged Brad back to the house, grumbling under my breath about my sandwich getting soggy, my shoulder aching, and the fact that I couldn't latch the gate properly with one hand. Not while blocking Brad out of it with my body and tugging on the gate at the same time. I finally gave up on the gate, satisfied when it stayed shut, and hauled the squealing baby into the house.

"Petey, you don't have to be so rough with him!"

"*You* don't have to be rough with him," I said, panting with effort and exasperation. "He won't come with me, and I can't pick him up and carry him."

"I'm sorry, Petey." Annie came to my rescue. "I forgot about your shoulder. Sit down and eat your sandwich. I'll clean him up before I get started in the kitchen."

She took the struggling baby into his room. I could hear her singing and talking to him to soothe him. I had really bruised his feelings. He was not a kid who liked being dragged around. I know better, too . . . I don't know what makes me do things like that, now and again.

I finished my milk and sandwich and was in the bathroom when I heard Annie sit down at the table with the baby. By now, he was laughing at some silly thing she was doing to amuse him.

Then the phone rang, and I knew from the conversation that it was Dad, wanting to talk to Mom.

"She's at Red's Service Station," Annie said. "She has a flat tire. They're going to patch it for her while she waits. The spare was flat, too."

Annie laughed at something Dad said. "But we're perfectly all right. We've been out in the pasture with the Chief. Now we're having snacks before I start supper for Mom. Anyway, Evan and T.C. will be along in a few minutes. Mom saw them pass the station in the jeep. Don't worry about us."

I tried to remember when Annie started calling him T.C., like the rest of us did, instead of Taro Chan. It must have been recently, because I hadn't noticed, before.

While Annie was still talking, I heard the door close softly. It wasn't T.C. and Evan coming in, because they would have made a lot more racket. I hadn't heard the jeep drive in. I hadn't latched the screen door, so I knew it must be Brad sneaking outside again. He would get right back into a mess.

It took me a minute to get my shirt buttoned and arranged. Then I started after him. I was in the kitchen when I heard the first yelp of the dogs.

18

For an instant, I couldn't move. Of course! Dogs! That was what I had heard while I was resting, earlier in the afternoon. Far off. Faint. Dogs hunting.

They had probably been in the Gopher Field, then casting around looking for the rest of the calves. Something had probably drawn them off, pulled them farther away from the house and out of earshot. A luckless rabbit, maybe. Or a deer.

Now they were back . . . out there in the yard. With the baby!

Then I could move. "Annie! The baby's outside!" I yelled, knowing that she must have heard the dogs. I didn't wait to see what she'd do. I didn't even think of how little I could do, in the shape I was in. I just hit the screen door with my good arm and came off the porch in two steps. I grabbed the broom as I ran past it.

Brad was screaming with fear. The pack—there must have been eight or nine dogs in it, though I didn't take time to count—had him backed up against the gate. They were looping and weaving around him, snapping at him now and again. There was a bloody gash on one side of his head as if one of the dogs had grabbed at an ear and missed its hold. There were other gashes on his fat legs and on the arms that he had instinctively held up before his face. Only the fact that he had set his heels stubbornly into the sand, pushing his back against the slats of the gate, had kept them from dragging him down.

The heifers weren't in sight, as I hurtled toward Brad. But the old Chief was on the other side of the gate. He was snorting and prancing, his ears back. The dogs paid no attention to him. He was too big for their use. They wanted something little. Something they could maul to death. Like Brad.

I landed in the middle of the pack, swinging the broom like a flail. A couple of good whacks sent the dogs backing off, startled. But they weren't through. They seemed to sense that there wasn't anything much that I could do to them. Perhaps they could see that I was wounded. Whatever it was, they decided that they could take me on, too. I could see it in their eyes. They started toward me, heads down, lips curled back over their teeth, the fur along their skinny backs standing up stiff. It was a thing I'll never forget as long as I live.

I've never been so scared. For the first time, I realized how futile the swinging broom handle was against a pack of determined and hungry dogs. I backed against the gate, squeezing the baby behind me against it, so the dogs couldn't get at him. I wedged him in tightly and kept swinging the broom. Suddenly, the gate that I hadn't been able to latch properly earlier gave way. Brad and I were dumped into the dust at the Chief's feet.

The dogs leaped forward as I fell, and I felt their teeth close on me. Especially my legs. I yelled and folded up around the baby as well as I could. I screamed again as one of the dogs sank his teeth into my bandaged shoulder.

That dog was suddenly lifted from the pack and flung, screaming, through the air. He landed in a sodden heap beside the fence. The old Chief was standing over us like a maddened shadow. He was striking out with his hooves, biting, kicking. He didn't look old, from where I lay curled in the dirt. He looked like a wild horse, his eyes red, his lips pulled back from his gums. Sounds came out of him that I'd never heard a horse make, not even in the movies. Sounds I never wanted to hear again.

He fought as I'd imagined wild stallions fought off wolf packs on the plains, in centuries past. Yet, although he seemed to be standing directly over us, he never so much as nicked us with one of his hooves.

The only thing that touched me was his tail, which snapped across my face when he whirled to meet some new threat from the dogs.

Three of the dogs were down, unmoving. The others started to back away, raging, fearful now of the horse. The Chief snaked his head along the ground, his legs set wide, balancing so as to meet his attackers from any direction. He challenged them again with one of those deep, whistling screams, and the dogs broke. They began to back away, snarling.

With everything that had happened right on top of me, I hadn't heard the jeep drive up. But now T.C. and Evan were there. T.C. had Dad's rifle. I saw a black-and-tan hound leap into the air and collapse before I heard the first shot. With the second, a red hound plunged forward, his front legs seeming to melt under him, his bloodied muzzle digging a furrow into the loose, pawed dirt. The Chief squealed again, snaking his head toward the three remaining dogs. They took off running for the woods. T.C. shot twice more, and only one dog disappeared into the trees.

The Chief stood snapping his mane from side to side for a moment longer. Then he visibly relaxed and came over to sniff at me, seeing if I was all right before walking out of the gate to see about Annie. He actually seemed to be checking us all out.

I hadn't even thought about Annie. She was in the fight, too. Now she was sitting in the dirt with tears running down her face. Her forearm was a bloody mess, where one of the dogs must have grabbed her when she waded in to help me. She wasn't quite as chewed as the baby and I were, because by the time she had told Dad what was happening, the Chief was taking care of a lot of the action.

"He fought them off," she said to nobody in particular in a funny, tight voice. "He fought them off."

"Annie, are you all right?" T.C.'s naturally pale face was altogether without color. He didn't seem to have any features except his very black eyes and the two smudgy lines of his eyebrows. The rest was just a blur.

"That was some shooting," Evan said. He put his hand on T.C.'s back. I think he was tactfully steadying him.

"Four in four shots," Annie said in the same funny voice. Her eyes were wide as she looked at T.C.

"I'm sorry, Annie. It's something I learned a long time ago."

"I'm not sorry," she whispered fiercely. "I'm not sorry at all!" She took his hand and came over to where I sat in the dirt holding the screaming baby. "They would have killed us, if it hadn't been for you and the Chief. He fought them off, and you shot them."

Evan looked at the dogs that the Chief had tossed away. "Look," he said as he touched the dog. Its head lolled limply. "He broke their backs as he tossed them off."

Annie shuddered. "I want to go into the house. T.C., would you bring the baby?" She didn't wait to see if he did, or even to look at me to see how badly I was chewed up. She just walked into the house, holding her bleeding right arm with her left hand.

Evan and T.C. looked at each other and then at me. "Shock," T.C. said. "She'll be all right, Petey. It's something that happens after a battle, sometimes. Can you walk?"

"Sure," I grunted. I tried to stand, after he lifted Brad out of my arms. My shoulder kind of exploded, and my stomach turned over a couple of times. I sat back down. "In a minute, maybe."

"Maybe, nothing," Evan said. He slid an arm around my back, being careful of my shoulder, and the other arm under my knees. He lifted me as easily as T.C. had picked up the baby. It would have been humiliating if I hadn't felt so weak.

I looked back over his shoulder at the Chief, as he carried me away. Now he didn't look like a wild horse. He looked old. Older than he ever had. He turned and walked toward his shed, where the little heifers waited. He stumbled as he walked.

"Should I take Petey up to his room?" Evan asked T.C.

"No," I said. "I don't want to get blood all over the sheets."

"Forget the sheets," T.C. snapped.

"No, really!" I insisted. "Put me down by the table. You can clean up the mess better there."

"I think we'd better take the three of you to the doctor, right away," Evan said.

Annie met us at the door. "T.C., you hold the baby while I see how badly he's hurt. Evan, you can clean up Petey, can't you?" She had already washed her arm and wrapped some gauze tightly around it as a compress.

There were bandages on the table, where she had them ready, as well as antiseptic. She took over, washing the baby with light dabs of clean cotton, talking to him, trying to quiet his cries enough to tell if he was really hurt or just frightened. Once or twice, she glanced my way or looked at T.C. Her expression was odd—sort of round-eyed.

I couldn't pay much attention to her. I had troubles of my own. Evan was as gentle as he could be, dabbing at the dirt and blood with antiseptic-dampened gauze. But it burned something fierce, and some of the gashes in my legs were deep. The pants were a total loss, unless we cut them off at the hips and used them for a bathing suit.

"Little buddy, you're going to need some major repairs on those legs," Evan said. "How about your shoulder? The bandage is all bloody. Did one of them get you there?"

"Yeah," I said, remembering how the Chief had grabbed that dog and flung him through the air. "He didn't have time to bite through to hurt," I said, between clenched teeth, "but I think the Chief pulled him off before he worried his way through the bandage."

There was the sound of cars outside, and Dad's feet hit the porch, almost before the engine died. Mom was half a step behind him. She gave a funny cry when she saw what a mess we all were in. She grabbed up the baby, who started wailing at the top of his voice all over again.

Annie told them the story. The boys filled in the details, because about then I was feeling light-headed again. I didn't remember until later that it was Evan who carried me outside and climbed into the back of the pickup, still holding me in his arms. T.C. got in back with us, and Annie and Mom, still clutching Brad, went into the cab with Dad.

We met the sheriff at our front gate. He didn't even wave us down, just took one look and whirled his car around in the road. He passed us with his siren blaring and his red lights flashing. Dad moved up to his back bumper and stayed right with him all the way to the hospital. It was the kind of ride I'd like to take sometime when I feel like enjoying it.

The sheriff must have radioed ahead, because there were doctors and nurses waiting on the emergency ramp when we pulled up to the hospital. Somebody shoved a needle full of sedative into me before I had time to object. What happened after that, I can't say.

19

I felt cold. I had been sitting out on a wild, nighttime prairie, and there was a campfire, but it wasn't giving out any heat. Only a blue, flickering light. The reason I was cold was that all my clothes were gone. A piece of stiff animal skin with hair on it was wrapped around my middle and hung almost to my knees. It would have been funny, except that there were other people around the fire, and all the men had on the same kind of rig. I looked again. The ladies did, too.

Nobody was saying anything, just passing around some roasted bones and grunting at each other. I wanted a bone, too, but they wouldn't offer me one. I was scared to ask.

One of the men threw his bone into the fire and made a "listen" sign. Suddenly, the whole bunch of us were surrounded by silent wolves. Great gray wolves, with little slanty red eyes and long, yellow teeth that showed when they rolled their snarling lips back. Everybody pulled in closer and closer to the fire. One by one, they disappeared into the flames, leaving me alone in the wolf circle.

I picked up the bone somebody had dropped and held it like a club, knowing that it was no weapon at all, just a gesture. It turned soft in my hands, dripping off my fingers like an ice-cream cone in summertime.

From out of the darkness, the old Chief thundered up. Not old anymore. Not ugly and bony. As he must have been, young and wild, on the plains. He flung himself among the wolves, biting, kicking, screaming. The suddenness of his appearance was too much for me. I fell back into the fire.

The cold fire wasn't cold anymore. Now it was intensely hot, searing my shoulder. I tried to get away from the flames, but I couldn't move. I kept calling to the Chief to come and get me, but he was too busy fighting the wolves to hear.

Then the wolves were gone, as silently as they had come. Gone. The Chief was holding on to my arm with his lips—the good arm, not the burning one— shaking it gently. He let go and reached up to lip my cheek with his soft, velvet muzzle. Then he faded into the darkness. The Chief was gone. I was alone.

"Pete. Pete! It's all right now, Petey. It's all right. Wake up. You're having a bad dream." Dad's voice came through at last.

I opened my eyes, blinking to bring things into focus. I clutched his hand tightly. "Dad?" My voice sounded funny, even to me.

"Right here, Pete."

"Where are we?"

"In the hospital. You guys were chewed up pretty bad. They've practically given over a whole floor to Braedens."

"Where's T.C.? And Evan? Were they chewed up, too?"

"No. They're fine. They're home, taking care of things. Mom wouldn't leave you kids for anything, and neither would I. Mom's down in the next room with Annie and Brad."

"I want to see them. The baby looked awful. His ear was cut."

"Not just cut, Pete. Pretty nearly torn off. But that Jerry Tucker is a good doctor. All the time he was stitching you up, he was showing me how he was putting the skin together so the scars won't be too bad, when you've healed. Annie and Brad are all right, Pete. Really."

"I want to see," I insisted.

"It's about three in the morning. If I push you down the hall now, some white-skirted bureaucrat is going to descend on us. Can you wait until morning?"

"I guess so. If you're sure they're all right."

"They are. Thanks to you. You got the worst of it, brudder."

"I couldn't do anything," I said, remembering with shame how futile the broomstick had been against the raging dogs. "If the Chief hadn't been there . . ." I didn't finish. The dogs and wolves of my dream suddenly melted together, and I shuddered. "I was dreaming about it."

"I know," Dad said. "The old Chief must have been something else, out there."

"He was great, Dad. I'll never tease Annie by calling him Dogmeat again. He looked like a wild stallion. He stood right over us and never touched us with a hoof while he was whirling around and fighting off the dogs."

"Annie told us. She also said you went off the porch and waded into the dog pack as if you'd been the U.S. fleet. The Chief couldn't get at them until you opened the gate. Annie grabbed the gun and brought it out, but the dogs were all over you, and she couldn't get a clear shot. She was using it like a club when T.C. grabbed it away from her. By then the Chief had driven them back, and he could get a good shot."

The door opened quietly, letting in the brighter light from the hall. A nurse put her head in and said, "Mr. Braeden, the sheriff is here."

"It's all right," Dad said. "Petey is awake. Ask him to come in."

She pulled her head back, and the sheriff came into the room. He walked softly, for such a big man.

"How goes it?" he asked me, with a nod in Dad's direction.

"I'll be all right. All right, that is, for somebody that was almost dogmeat."

"Too bad that had to happen," he said, looking at Dad. "But sometimes it takes a near tragedy to get results. I've been on the phone to our state representative. The next time we get up a petition in this county to outlaw deer packs and to make people keep their hounds penned, he won't dare to shelve it, as he did the last one. That's been our main problem. The only way to stop it is by state law. The representative runs his own pack of hounds, and he just doesn't listen real good to the people who want it stopped. I'm going to count on you to help get signatures on our petitions."

"You know you have it," Dad said. "Plus anything else you need. That one pack won't bother anybody else, but there are a dozen other ones out in the woods, worrying the wildlife. Probably the livestock, too."

The sheriff shook his head. "I doubt that there are a dozen packs that run loose like that. Most folks keep 'em up. But the day of the deer hound is about over. It's a shame, in a way. At one time, people needed dogs to trail for them in these deep woods, to bring out the game. It's a tradition . . . used to be a necessity, when folks had to have venison for meat. Now most of the deep woods are gone, and using dogs is dirty pool."

"We see a deer, now and again, on our place. Not

as many as Susan remembers when she was young," Dad said.

"Not all that many left," the sheriff said. "Over-hunted. Too many people with guns. Not enough woods. These big rifle clubs keep yelling about keeping down the overpopulation of deer. I don't know how it is in other counties, but overpopulation is no problem here. If it keeps on the way it's going, pretty soon, there won't be any deer at all. Be extinct, like the dodo."

"Did you get anyone to claim those dogs?" Dad asked.

"Oh, they were Blackburn's, all right. He'll be over to see you in the morning. He'll pay damages for the calves. Pay these hospital bills, too, I expect." His smile had no humor in it, and I decided I wouldn't want him mad at me.

"Would he have paid for the funeral, if the dogs had killed one of my people?" Dad asked, his voice grim.

The sheriff didn't answer, just shook his head. "He said he had a young Morgan horse—colt, rather—that he was going to give your girl, to replace the old horse."

A big, cold icicle laid itself right along my backbone and set me to shaking. I looked at Dad and saw the tightness in his face. My voice came out in a whisper. "What happened to the Chief? He's dead, isn't he?"

Dad nodded, slowly. "Kurt took the boys out to the farm, after we saw you were going to be all right.

They went out to see the Chief. He was down on the straw in his shed. The little heifers were snuggled up all around him as if they were trying to keep him warm."

I didn't say anything. The tears rolled out of my eyes. I didn't try to stop them. I just kept feeling the soft velvet of his muzzle on my cheek when he came to say good-bye.

"Pete." Dad touched me lightly on the good shoulder. "Pete, don't feel bad about him. He put out everything he had, fighting off the dogs, because you were his people. His old heart had been beating for a long time. It just couldn't take a strain like that. There wasn't enough left to keep it going."

"Does Annie know yet?" I managed to ask.

"I wanted to tell you both in the morning," Dad answered.

"Maybe I'd better tell her," I said. "Early, before someone lets it slip."

The sheriff shifted uncomfortably. "Sorry about that, Pete. I thought you knew."

"I think you're right, Pete. You're the best one to tell Annie. If you don't mind," Dad said.

"No, I don't mind," I said. I closed my eyes.

Dad and the sheriff went outside and talked in voices I couldn't quite hear. When Dad came back into the room, I pretended to be dozing. He sat in the big chair beside the bed and dropped off to sleep, snoring softly.

I lay there, thinking about the dogs and the Chief. I felt as if I had swallowed a Popsicle whole, and it was lodged with the cold part in my stomach and the two little sticks stabbing me in the heart. The pain was worse than the dog bites on my legs. The doctor had given me a shot for those.

There wasn't any easy cure for this pain. I lay there with my throat burning, tears stinging my eyelids and rolling hotly down my temples.

Was it stupid to cry over a dumb old dogmeat horse that wasn't even mine? In the end, he'd been mine as much as anybody's. Anyway, he thought I was his, which is about the same thing, isn't it?

I lay there and tried to think how I was going to tell Annie. And wished that daylight would come. After a while, I slept.

20

Dad had gone, when I woke. A nurse came in and started stirring things up. When she brought my breakfast tray, Dad came with it.

"Annie's in much better shape than you are, Pete. The doctor is going to let her go home this morning. But she'll be in to see you, as soon as she finishes her breakfast."

"Could she come eat with me?" I asked.

"Can't think of any good reason why not. I'll ask," he said. He disappeared again.

In a couple of minutes, the door opened. Annie came in, pushing her bed tray before her. "Dad said you wanted company. How do you feel?"

"I hurt," I said, with complete honesty.

"The rest of us are going home this morning. Are you coming too? You look awful."

"Thanks a lot," I said. "How would I know? They don't tell me things like that."

"You must not hurt much. You're grouchy."

"I'm not grouchy. I have a lot on my mind."

"What mind?" Annie chuckled.

"All right," I said. "All right. Are you going to eat or fight?"

She laughed and took the silver lid off her eggs. "Petey, you really are a dumb kid. What made you wade into those dogs like that?"

I pushed my eggs around on the plate. "I didn't stop to think how dumb it was. I couldn't stand there and do nothing. Anyway, it never occurred to me that dogs would really attack a person. I never expected it. The dogs I know don't bite people."

I took a bite of the eggs and put the fork down. "Besides, it's like they say in the cowboy shows—'a man has to do what a man has to do.' "

Annie laughed at me. Not making fun, a serious kind of laugh. "I wasn't all that smart, myself. Even if I'd known how to use that gun, there was no way to get a shot. There was just a big tumble of boys and dogs . . . until that gate came open. How did you get it open, anyway?"

"It wasn't latched. I couldn't fasten it right when I dragged Brad up to the house. It was just kind of caught by friction. I thought we were goners, when it opened up behind, and we fell down."

"Goners!" Annie snorted. "I never saw anything

171

like the Chief. He just seemed to go wild. When you hollered, he picked up one of those dogs, shook it, and threw it thirty feet away. I never saw anything so magnificent. I even dreamed about it last night."

She sounded so proud and excited that I felt all sinky inside. "So did I. Only it was wolves instead of dogs. It was like a long time ago, and he was a wild horse. When he drove the wolves off, he lipped me on the face and kind of faded away." My voice faded and cracked.

Annie studied me. "What's the matter, Petey? Something's wrong with the Chief?"

I nodded. "His heart was too old, Annie. He fought with everything he had. There wasn't anything left when he had driven the dogs off."

"Oh, Pete!" Annie said. She didn't cry or anything. Not then. With her hand shaking, she put the lid back on the cold eggs and shoved the bed table away. For a little while, she stood looking out of the window at the little park on the hospital grounds, where the squirrels played in the early morning sunshine. Finally, she turned back to me. "Petey, when did Dad tell you?"

"Last night. He was going to tell both of us this morning, but the sheriff came by and let it slip. I wanted to tell you. I didn't do it very well, did I?"

She moved away from the window and hitched herself up onto the bed beside me. She sat, legs dangling. "You did O.K., Petey. There isn't any good way." Then she just sat, not looking at anything. Sitting still.

After a bit, I said, "You O.K.?"

"Yeah. I'm O.K. I was just thinking about things—how everybody laughed when I bought him. Now, when nobody would make fun of him anymore, he's dead."

"Do you really care?" I asked, not quite believing that all that mattered to her was what other people thought. "Do you really and truly care what they think?"

Annie looked at me. Her face was solemn. "Maybe I care too much about what others think. Not enough about what I think and what the people I love think."

"I think you think too much," I said.

"I think you're right." Annie cuffed me lightly on the good arm. Then she asked, "Petey, do you like me anymore?"

"That's a dumb question. You're my sister. Of course I like you."

"It's just that we haven't been close like we used to be. Before we moved. Before T.C. came."

"We were little kids in San Francisco, before Dad came home. We're not kids anymore. I don't feel a bit like a kid."

"I don't either. I haven't for a long time. Don't you miss San Francisco, Petey?"

"Sure. I miss some of my friends there. Tommy Roberson was the best friend I ever had. I miss him. Some of the others, too, but nobody as much as Tommy."

"I know. I've tried to make new friends here. It

hasn't worked very well. They're nice enough to me, but I don't feel about them the way I did about some of those we left."

"Tanya and Cathy and that bunch? They're B.I.P.'s, Annie. Born in Pine Hill. You won't ever fit into their crowd, not really. You've seen too much of the world, been too many places to think small, like they do. You know what's out in the world . . . more than they do, anyway. You're bigger than they are, inside. You won't ever feel easy with them."

She reached over and hugged me, very carefully. "Thanks, Petey. Still, I've acted pretty small, sometimes. Like with T.C."

"You sure have . . . but you're still nice people. Dad says it just takes time to get to know each other, sometimes."

"And I don't like living on the farm much, either. Or I didn't. Now I'm not sure. I don't like the way Mom has changed. She never has time for us anymore."

"To play, the way we used to, you mean? Like she does with Brad? We don't need for her to play with us anymore. Not like that. We're not babies, Annie. Brad is. And Mom works all the time, in the house and the garden and driving the tractor when they're hauling hay. You could do that for her."

"I can't drive."

"I can. You can learn. Things are going pretty good now. We can do lots of things together now. Fishing, picnics, that kind of thing."

"And riding horses." She looked down at her hands.

"And riding horses. You can still get a riding horse. The Chief wasn't what you needed for that."

"No. But if I hadn't bought him, I might not have either of my little brothers, today," Annie said. "I'm not sorry about the horse I bought. I'll never regret that."

"The sheriff said Mr. Blackburn might give you a horse. A Morgan colt."

"I'm not sure I want another horse, right now, Petey. I'm not sure I need a horse anymore."

"You're a nut," I said. "A real nut."

"You just might be right. A little green nut with the shell all tight up around it. All the doors closed."

"So now what?"

"Open the doors, I guess." She shook her head from side to side. "Or try to."

"What about Tanya and that bunch of snobs?"

"They're not really snobs. Like you said, they haven't been around much. They're covering that up. What do you think of Brenda?"

"She's no glamor girl like Tanya. She's too fat, but she looks at things straight on, and she isn't all the time making fun of people. I don't like people to make fun of other people."

"Neither do I, Petey. And I didn't like them making fun of the Chief, either. Especially not of him."

"What'll they do with him?" I asked. "Bury him, like they did the dead calves?"

"I guess so. I suppose Daddy will take care of that."

"Daddy will take care of what?" Mom asked from the doorway.

"You know . . . burying the Chief," Annie said.

"Are you all right, Annie?"

"Sure, just sad."

"Your father talked with T.C. a few minutes ago. He and Evan have made a grave for the Chief under that big pine tree. They haven't closed it up yet. T.C. thought you might like to say good-bye."

Annie slid off the bed. "I sure would."

"So would I," I said, throwing back the covers.

"Not you, Pete. You and the baby are going to stay put for a day or two. Dr. Tucker wants you here so he can keep an eye on you."

"I feel all right," I lied, trying not to wince when I let my legs slide over the edge of the bed. "Anyway, it was me he fought for. I think I've got a right to be there."

Kids don't have many rights in some families, but mine isn't one of those. Dad came in, just then, and nodded in my direction. "If the doctor wants Pete back, I'll bring him back. He does have a right to be there, if he feels like making the trip."

And that settled that.

He went off to get the doctor's O.K. and came back with a pair of pants for me. I don't know where he got them. They were four sizes too big. That was a good thing, though, because they went over the bundlesome bandages on my legs without binding the way jeans would have. I had to wad them up around

176

my waist and pull my belt tight to keep them on. Since Dad picked me up out of the wheelchair and put me into the truck, I didn't do anything like standing around, so there wasn't much danger of losing them. Mom stayed at the hospital with Brad, and just Dad and Annie and I went to say good-bye to the Chief.

21

Nobody talked much. Dad looked straight ahead at the road, paying more attention to his driving than he needed to. Annie fiddled with the edges of her cutoffs, fringing them deeper. I leaned my head against the cool glass of the pickup window and thought about the Chief.

He had been old and unrideable, but there had been a certain grace about him, an air of force that had extended beyond what he was to what he had been. Yesterday, I hadn't seen a sagging old dogmeat horse. I'd seen a wild, free pony from the plains of Montana, a well-trained cutting horse, the wise and beautiful Indian Pony of the sideshow. All that he had been had showed in the way he moved, giving every bit of himself to protecting Brad and me from the dogs.

I don't think he even knew he was a horse. He was just my friend. I know that's crazy, but that's what I was thinking.

T.C. came out to meet us.

"Where's Evan?" Dad asked, nodding toward the jeep.

"He stayed with me today. We called for permission. The principal's office said it would be all right, if you called later, and we made up our work."

Dad smiled at him and looked around.

T.C. smiled back at him. "Evan is out with the Chief. We didn't leave him."

Annie gave him a strange look, but she didn't say anything.

It embarrassed T.C. He seemed to want to explain to her. "When someone, something, fights beside you, dies for you, he deserves more than . . ." He let the sentence drift off lamely, not knowing how to finish it.

Annie put her hand on his arm, very lightly. "I understand. Thank you for making him a place and for waiting for me."

T.C. stumbled over his feet getting out of her way and opening the gate, so we could go over to where Evan sat beside the huge mound of earth.

Dad came around the pickup and took me off the seat as if I didn't weigh almost a hundred pounds and he didn't have a bad leg. He seemed pleased about something. He wasn't nearly as sad as the occasion demanded.

"What are you grinning about?" I whispered.

He wiped the grin from the corners of his mouth, but not from his eyes. "Annie and T.C.," he hissed back at me. "I think she really looked at him for the first time, just now."

Which was a strange thing to say, since T.C. had been living with us for more than a year.

Dad put me down at the edge of the grave, so I could see in. The dreadful sight I'd been expecting wasn't there. The Chief wasn't all stiff and bloated in death. Instead, he looked as if he were asleep, his haunches pulled up under, his front hooves folded under his chest, like a big, contented cat. His head was stretched out in front, eyes closed.

The boys had made a bed of thick, fragrant alfalfa hay to put him on. His mane and tail had been brushed to fine silk and spread out on the straw like the fringe of a Japanese cushion. The drooping underlip didn't show, now. He looked young, as he had yesterday in the fight. Young and sleeping.

"I don't suppose one prays over animals," Dad said softly, his hand on Annie's shoulder. "Just the same, I've been saying prayers of thanks that he was here when we needed him."

"He looks beautiful," Annie said, with a quiver in her voice. "But he was always beautiful to me."

Evan handed Annie the Indian saddle blanket and

180

the beaded bridle. "We started to put these on him, but we didn't know if you would want us to."

"They're his," she said, touching the rough blanket lightly with the palm of her hand.

Evan slid down the lower side of the hole carefully and shook out the blanket, spreading it over the Chief. It wasn't big enough to cover all of him, but it went over his head and the forepart of his body. Then he laid the beaded bridle beside the blanket and climbed out of the grave.

"Why don't you wait up at the house, Annie?" he asked. "T.C. and I will finish here."

She nodded. There were tears squeezing out around the dark fringes of her eyelashes. Annie never liked for anyone to see her cry. She walked away, not toward the house but to the shed, where the four Angus heifers huddled together, disconsolate.

I pushed myself up. "I'm going with Annie," I said, but I made only two steps before my legs buckled. It was a stupid feeling, not to be able to stand up. Dad put his arms around my shoulders, careful of the bad one.

"Want me to carry you?"

"No. I want to walk, if you'll help me."

"That's what I'm here for," he said without smiling.

Annie didn't look up when we came near, though she must have heard us. She had shaken oats out of the bucket for the heifers. Flakes of oats lay like snow on their curly black foreheads. Annie bent over them, dusting the oats off as they ate, talking softly.

"I'm not going to cry," she said. "I'm not going to cry."

"Why not, sweetie?" Dad asked her. "There's a time for crying."

She buried her face in the furry back of the nearest calf and sobbed as if her heart were breaking. My own throat swelled, and my eyes burned. But I'd already cried my tears for the Chief. I sat back against the fence and let Dad handle this. I never knew what to do when girls cried.

"It isn't fair," Annie sobbed. "It just isn't fair."

Dad looked at me with a sad smile. We'd already had this conversation. He went over to Annie and held her against his chest, rubbing the back of her neck, smoothing the tensions away. "What isn't fair, sweetie?"

"Oh, Daddy. Everything. He didn't have a chance to have a real home. All those years of wandering around. I wanted him to have a home."

Dad was silent for a time, just rubbing Annie's neck gently and patting her on the back. Finally, he held her away from him, so she had to look up at him.

"Annie, nobody ever said life was fair. It isn't. There's nothing fair about it."

Annie wasn't crying so hard, now. She was sniffling some and trying to regain control.

"Honey, Life or Nature or whatever it's called isn't cruel or wicked or kind. It's just relentless. Everything that is born must grow and die. Some sooner, some later. Everything dies. The Chief had a lot of good years. He might have had a few more, but he did something for us in a few days that all the future years could never equal."

"Do you think he knew it'd kill him to fight like that?" Annie asked.

Dad shook his head. "No. Only man knows things like that. Everything else just lives every minute of every day it has. Animals have no way of anticipating death. When the end comes, it comes. No fear. No regret."

"How do you know?" Annie sniffled.

Dad shrugged. "You'll know, too, someday." He let Annie's arms go and came to lean over the fence beside me. He looked very tired.

"Man knows. Sometimes an officer knows when he sends his men out that they'll never make it back. That's when it really hurts. We grieve for the ones who go, but we can't be angry with life, or with whatever god we worship. We have to accept the comings and goings and enjoy what time we have with each other."

"I wanted the Chief to have a home here and time to enjoy it."

Dad's smile was sad, his voice husky. " 'Home is the sailor, home from sea,/And the hunter home from the hill.' He was home, Annie. He knew it when he backed out of the trailer. He wasn't home long, but it was long enough."

The heifers finished the oats and began to jostle around Annie.

"All right now?" Dad asked her.

Annie sniffed once more, then chuckled. "I guess

so. For now. It's hard to cry when you've got a wet nose in your ear." She pushed the calf out of the way and came to stand beside us. "You O.K., Petey? You look like a ghost."

"I feel kinda spooky," I said. "I think I'd better lie down somewhere."

Dad picked me up. "I think you'd better get back to the hospital. I promised I'd bring you right back. You coming, Annie?"

She didn't answer, just looked toward the boys, who were still working with the tractor under the pine tree.

"You can still get another horse for this summer," Dad said, hesitantly, as if he didn't know if this was the time to broach the subject.

"I know, Daddy. But I don't think I need a horse anymore."

I could see the puzzlement on Dad's face. Annie saw it too and smiled at him. "I knew it when I bought the Chief. The Absolutely Perfect Horse is a dream. Something to fill in the empty places. A horse was something to get me into the group I wanted to be with at school. But I have other friends who don't have horses. Brenda doesn't. Evan doesn't."

"But you've wanted a horse forever, Annie," I said.

"I always wanted a horse who would do something wonderful for me. Make me popular, give me all kinds of excitement. Well, the horse I had gave me everything I asked for yesterday. It wasn't the way I planned it. But"—she shrugged—"are things ever like you plan them, Daddy?"

"Not very often, I'm afraid." Dad said.

"I know. I guess that's why I don't need a horse anymore. Petey said something about Mr. Blackburn giving me a Morgan colt. Even if he doesn't, Dr. Kurt will let me ride Dancer this summer. I would enjoy a ride, now and then."

"Maybe we could borrow two horses," I said.

"Why, Petey! I didn't think you liked horses!" She sounded surprised.

"I didn't," I said. "But I'm just a little kid. I can still change my mind, can't I?"

Dad shifted my weight and said, "You won't get to trade on that 'little kid' routine much longer, brudder. Annie, I have to take this invalid back to the hospital before the doctor comes looking for him. You'll be O.K.?"

The boys, finished with the grave, were walking toward us.

"I'll be just fine," Annie said, moving away toward them. She linked her arm with T.C.'s. "Come on up to the house, brudder. I'll bet you two guys haven't had a decent meal since yesterday."

I felt Dad give a deep sigh. A looked passed between him and T.C. that had more meanings than I could understand. But I understood enough to make me feel good inside.

Dad put me on the seat of the pickup and came around to the driver's side. He was grinning again and humming something off key under his breath.

"Now what are you grinning about?" I asked him.

He ruffled up my hair and pulled me over close

to him on the seat. "The phoenix is rising, brudder," he said. There was a laugh in his voice.

"I don't know what that means." I yawned. "But I'll think about it when I wake up."